TAO
The Little Samurai

pranks #1
and Attacks!

Laurent Richard
illustrated by Nicolas Ryser
Translation: Edward Gauvin

GRAPHIC UNIVERSE™ • MINNEAPOLIS

STORY BY LAURENT RICHARD
ILLUSTRATIONS BY NICOLAS RYSER
TRANSLATION BY EDWARD GAUVIN

FIRST AMERICAN EDITION PUBLISHED IN 2014 BY GRAPHIC UNIVERSE™.

FARCES ET ATTAQUES! BY LAURENT RICHARD AND NICOLAS RYSER © BAYARD ÉDITIONS, 2011
COPYRIGHT © 2014 BY LERNER PUBLISHING GROUP, INC., FOR THE US EDITION

GRAPHIC UNIVERSE™ IS A TRADEMARK OF LERNER PUBLISHING GROUP, INC.

GRAPHIC UNIVERSE™
A DIVISION OF LERNER PUBLISHING GROUP, INC.
241 FIRST AVENUE NORTH
MINNEAPOLIS, MN 55401 USA

FOR READING LEVELS AND MORE INFORMATION,
LOOK UP THIS TITLE AT WWW.LERNERBOOKS.COM.

MAIN BODY TEXT SET IN CCWILDWORDS 8.5/10.5.
TYPEFACE PROVIDED BY FONTOGRAPHER.

LIBRARY OF CONGRESS CATALOGING-IN-PUBLICATION DATA

RICHARD, LAURENT, 1968–
    [FARCES ET ATTAQUES! ENGLISH.]
    PRANKS AND ATTACKS! / LAURENT RICHARD ; ILLUSTRATED BY NICOLAS RYSER ; TRANSLATION,
EDWARD GAUVIN. – FIRST AMERICAN EDITION.
        P.   CM. – (TAO, THE LITTLE SAMURAI ; #1)
    SUMMARY: TAO IS A STUDENT AT MASTER SNOW'S MARTIAL ARTS SCHOOL. WITH HIS FRIENDS
RAY AND LEE AND HIS NOT-GIRLFRIEND KAT, HE TRIES TO FOLLOW THE TEACHINGS OF MARTIAL ARTS
MASTERS—OR, MORE OFTEN, FINDS A WAY AROUND THE MASTERS' ADVICE.
    ISBN 978-1-4677-2095-3 (LIB. BDG. : ALK. PAPER)
    ISBN 978-1-4677-2554-5 (EBOOK)
    1. GRAPHIC NOVELS. [1. GRAPHIC NOVELS. 2. MARTIAL ARTS–FICTION. 3. SAMURAI–FICTION.
4. SCHOOLS–FICTION. 5. BEHAVIOR–FICTION.] I. RYSER, NICOLAS, ILLUSTRATOR. II. GAUVIN,
EDWARD, TRANSLATOR. III. TITLE.
PZ7.7.R5PR 2014
741.5'944–DC23   2013027733

MANUFACTURED IN THE UNITED STATES OF AMERICA
1 – VI – 12/31/13

No Point Running Just to Be On Time

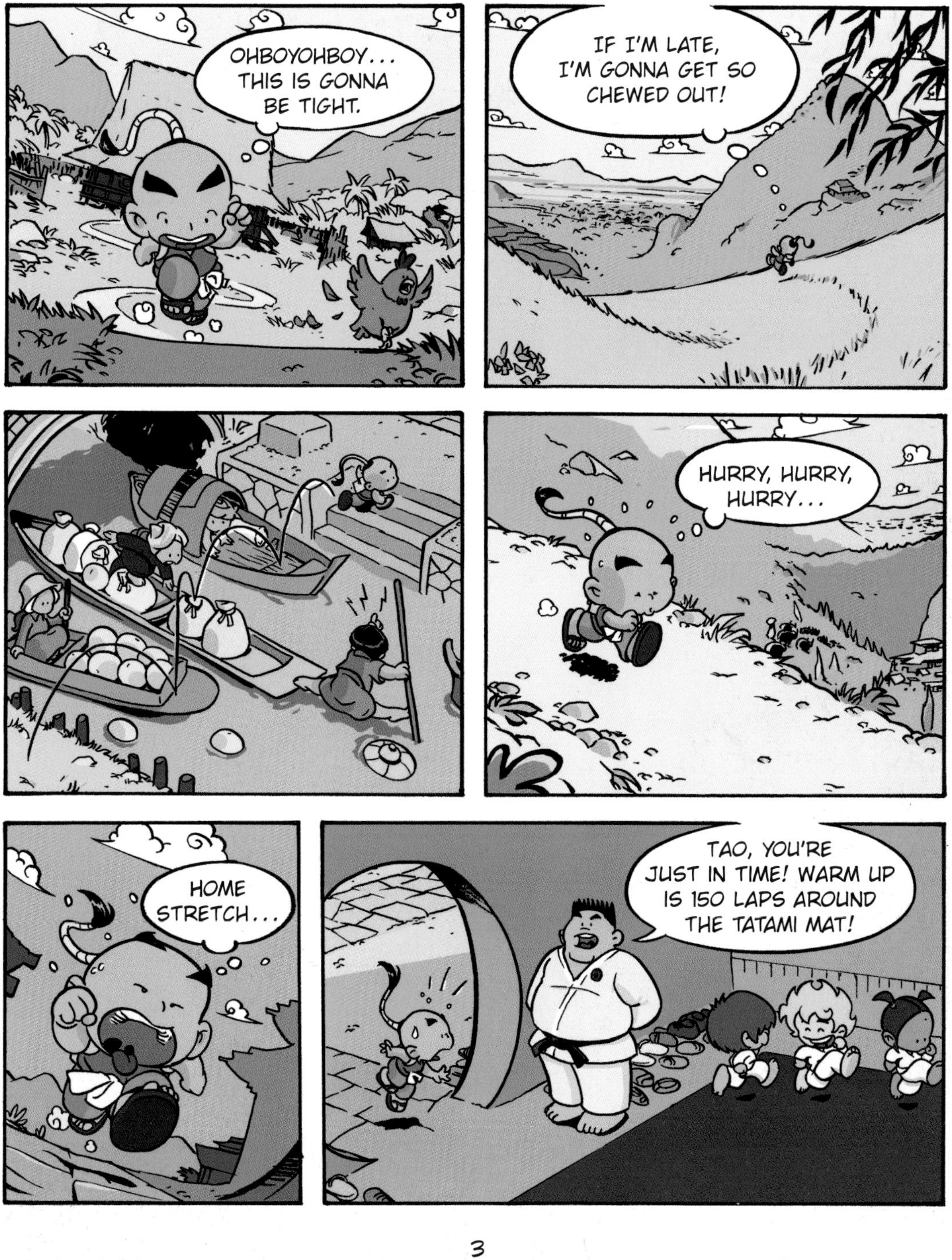
OHBOYOHBOY... THIS IS GONNA BE TIGHT.
IF I'M LATE, I'M GONNA GET SO CHEWED OUT!
HURRY, HURRY, HURRY...
HOME STRETCH...
TAO, YOU'RE JUST IN TIME! WARM UP IS 150 LAPS AROUND THE TATAMI MAT!

Showing Off Can Spoil Dessert

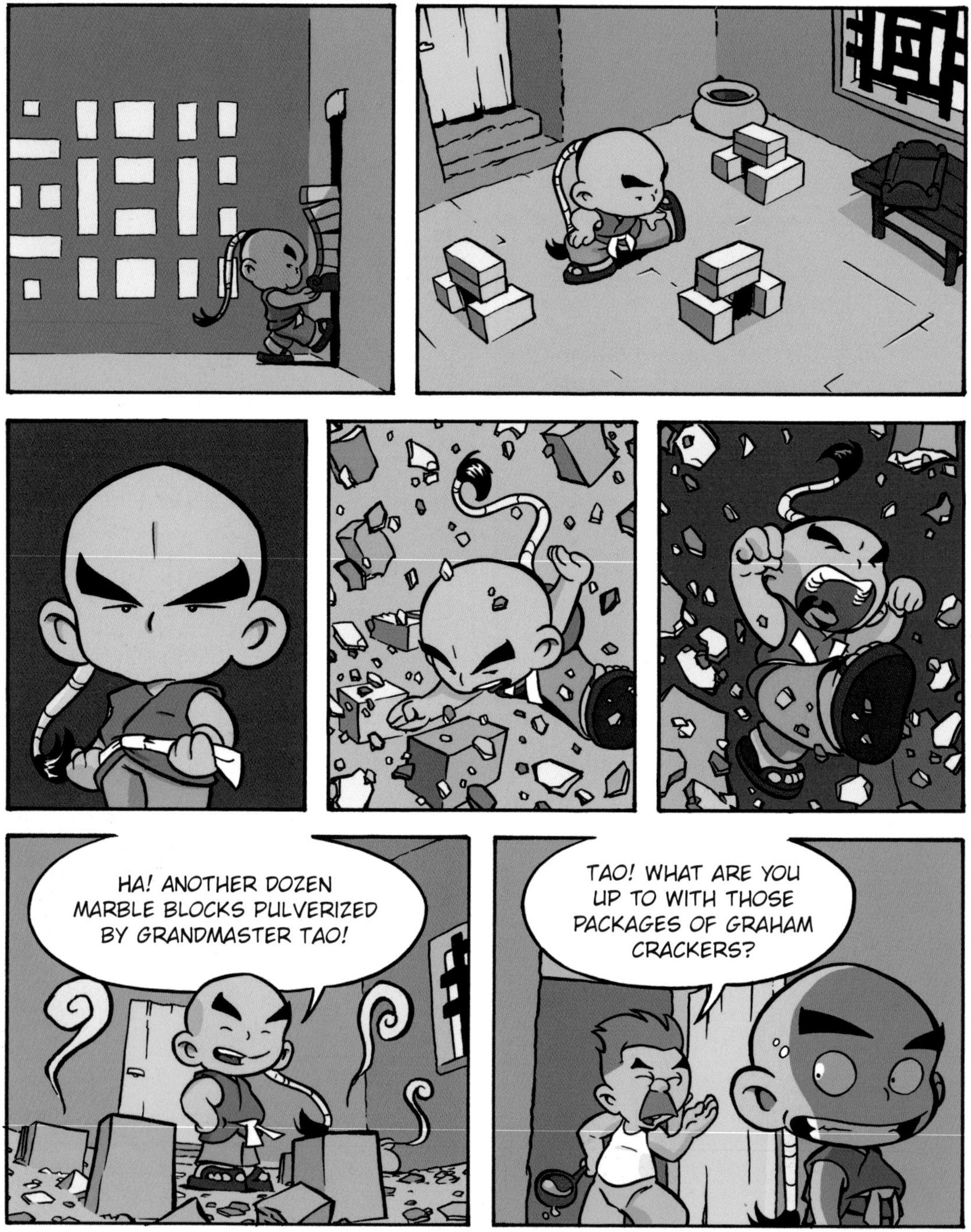
HA! ANOTHER DOZEN MARBLE BLOCKS PULVERIZED BY GRANDMASTER TAO!
TAO! WHAT ARE YOU UP TO WITH THOSE PACKAGES OF GRAHAM CRACKERS?

Clothes Don't Make the Samurai

THANKS FOR GIVING ME A HAND, KAT!

NO PROBLEM!

THIS HELMET'S AWKWARD! AND A SAMURAI'S OUTFIT IS SUPER IMPORTANT. I HAVE TO LOOK FIERCE!

BEWARE!

TAO, STOP WRIGGLING!

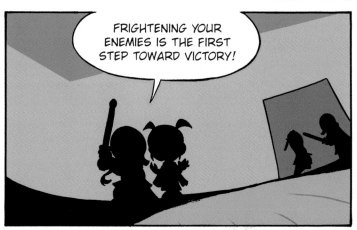

FRIGHTENING YOUR ENEMIES IS THE FIRST STEP TOWARD VICTORY!

TAO IS COMING. TREMBLE BEFORE ME!

WHAT'S SO FUNNY?

The Grasshopper's Cry Does Not Frighten the Lion

AAAAA
TAO, GOOD TO SEE YOU PRACTICING YOUR KIAI* OUTSIDE OF CLASS.
PRACTICE MAKES PERFECT.
UH . . . YEAH. IT'S JUST . . . MY HAIR GOT CAUGHT IN THE DOOR!
LITTLE HELP HERE?
?
PLEASE?

*KIAI: A SHORT YELL MADE BY MARTIAL ARTISTS BEFORE, DURING, OR AFTER A TECHNIQUE

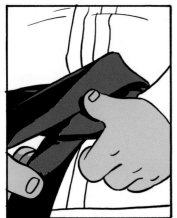

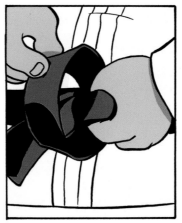

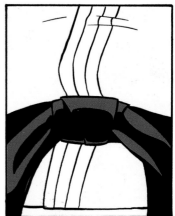

YOUR TURN. I'LL WATCH.

HMM... BETTER TRY AGAIN, TAO.

He Who Would See Far Must First Rise High

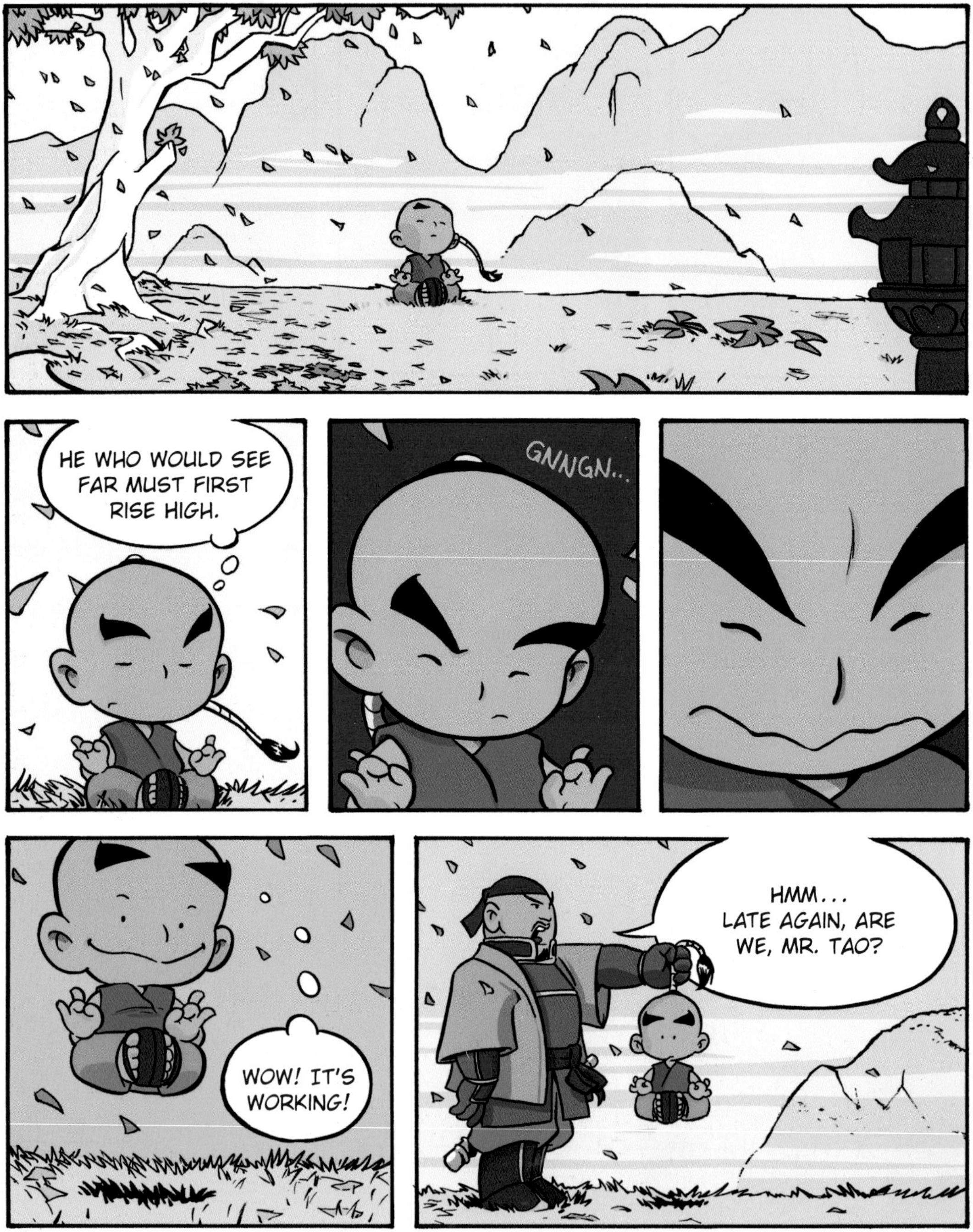
HE WHO WOULD SEE FAR MUST FIRST RISE HIGH.
GNNGN...
WOW! IT'S WORKING!
HMM... LATE AGAIN, ARE WE, MR. TAO?

The Master Shines, the Student Monkeyshines

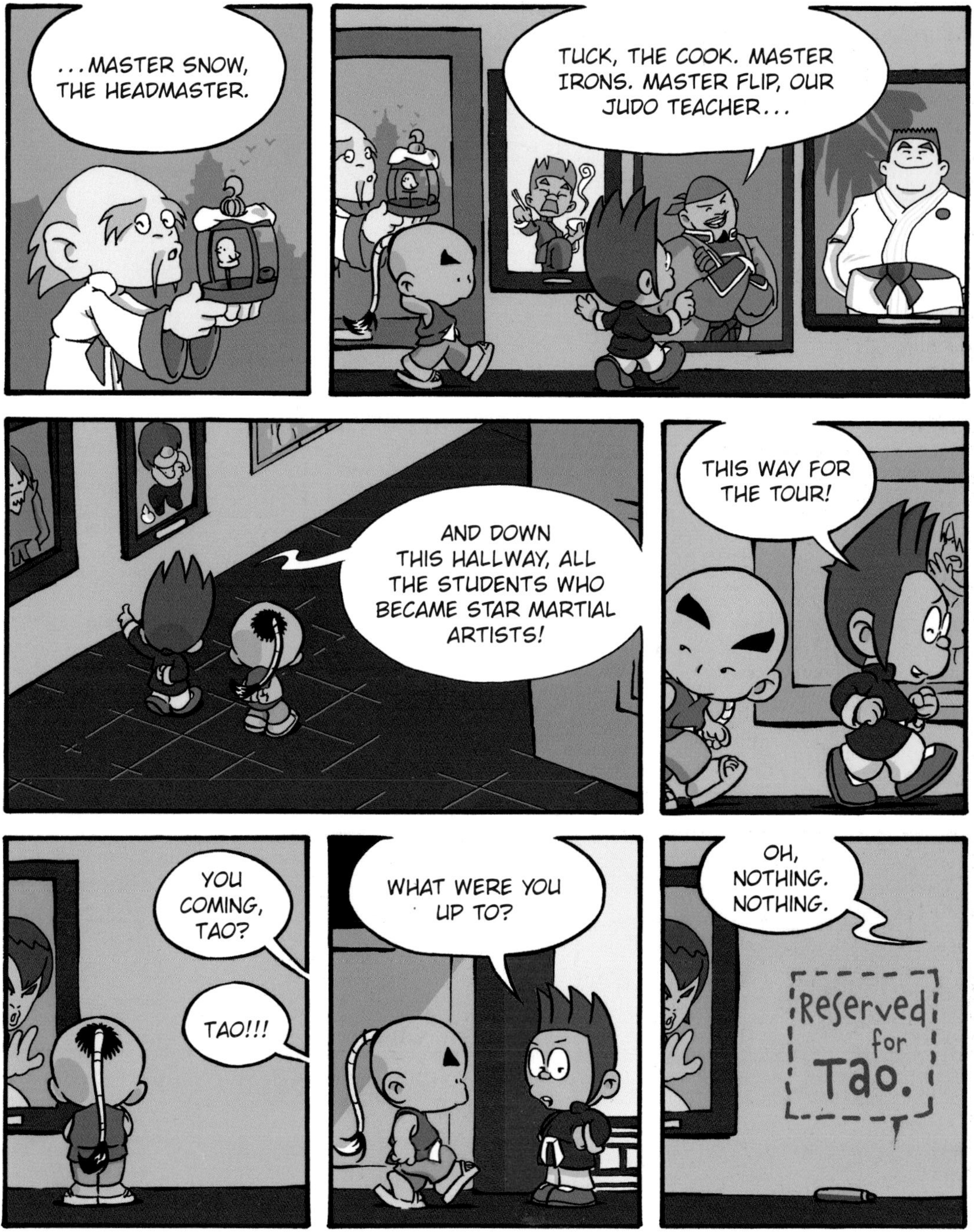

...MASTER SNOW, THE HEADMASTER.
TUCK, THE COOK. MASTER IRONS. MASTER FLIP, OUR JUDO TEACHER...
AND DOWN THIS HALLWAY, ALL THE STUDENTS WHO BECAME STAR MARTIAL ARTISTS!
THIS WAY FOR THE TOUR!
YOU COMING, TAO?
TAO!!!
WHAT WERE YOU UP TO?
OH, NOTHING. NOTHING.
Reserved for Tao.

He Who Climbs Too Fast Falls Flat on His Face

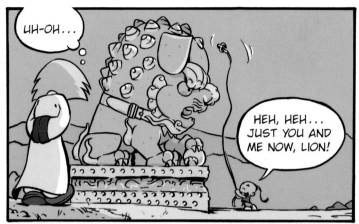

UH-OH...

HEH, HEH... JUST YOU AND ME NOW, LION!

CAREFUL, YOUNG TAO. THE LITTLE CAMEL MUST GROW BIG BEFORE IT CAN CLIMB MOUNTAINS!

CAMELS? WHAT IS HE TALKING ABOUT?

KRAK

WHOA--NO WAY! I'M TELEKINETIC!

When Zen Masters Lose Their Cool

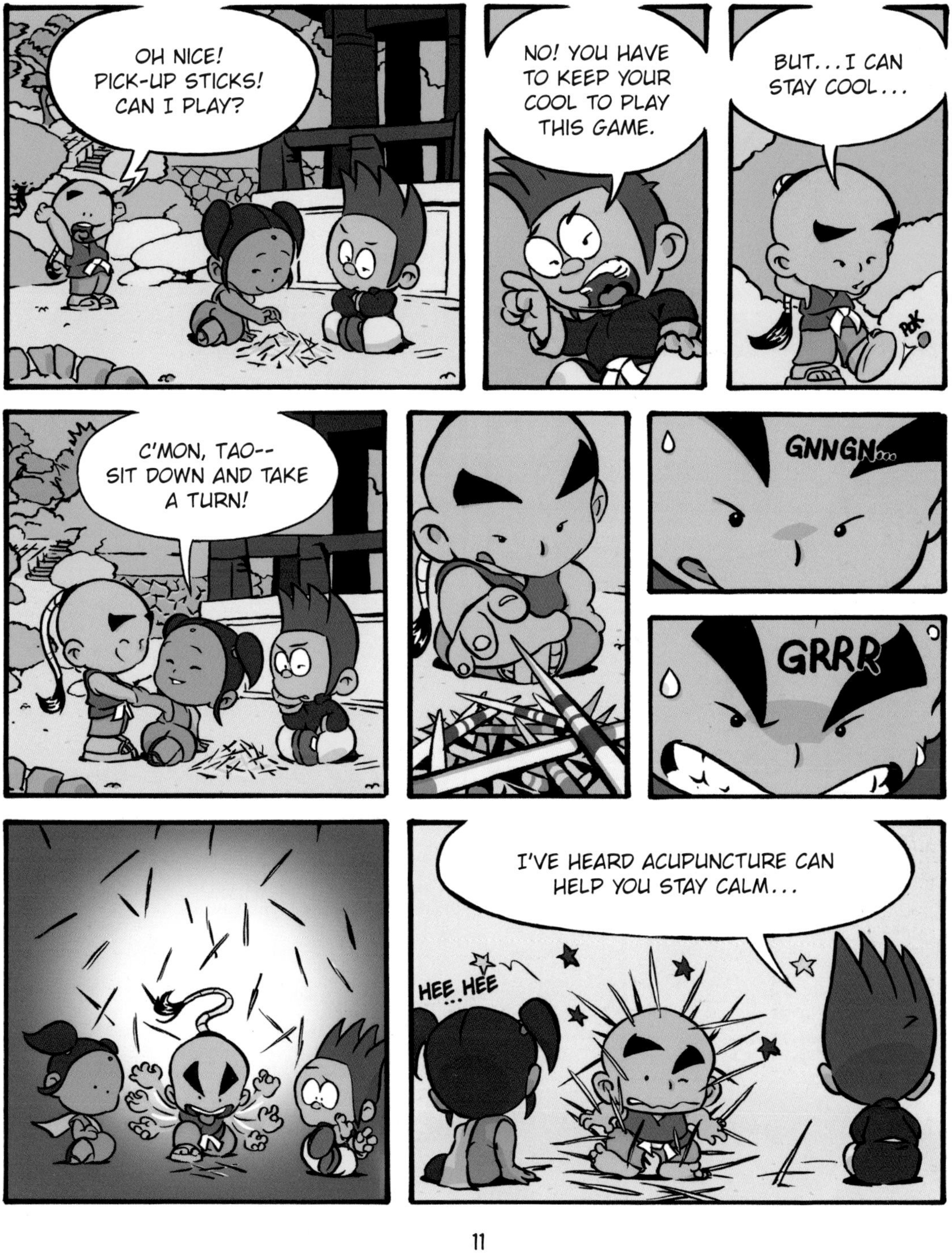

OH NICE! PICK-UP STICKS! CAN I PLAY?
NO! YOU HAVE TO KEEP YOUR COOL TO PLAY THIS GAME.
BUT... I CAN STAY COOL...
C'MON, TAO-- SIT DOWN AND TAKE A TURN!
GNNGN...
GRRR
HEE HEE...
I'VE HEARD ACUPUNCTURE CAN HELP YOU STAY CALM...

A Bird in the Fist

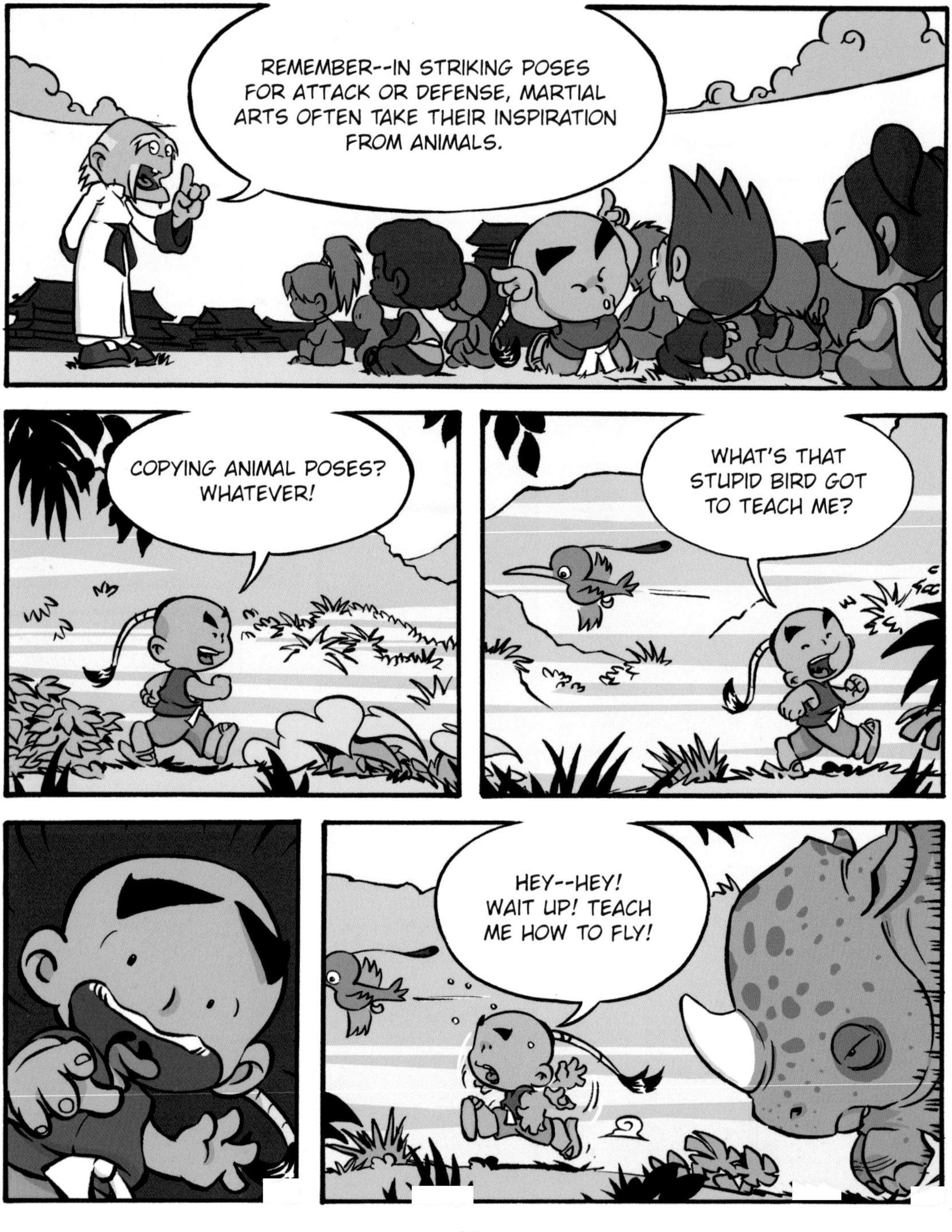
REMEMBER--IN STRIKING POSES FOR ATTACK OR DEFENSE, MARTIAL ARTS OFTEN TAKE THEIR INSPIRATION FROM ANIMALS.
COPYING ANIMAL POSES? WHATEVER!
WHAT'S THAT STUPID BIRD GOT TO TEACH ME?
HEY--HEY! WAIT UP! TEACH ME HOW TO FLY!

Snack Attack

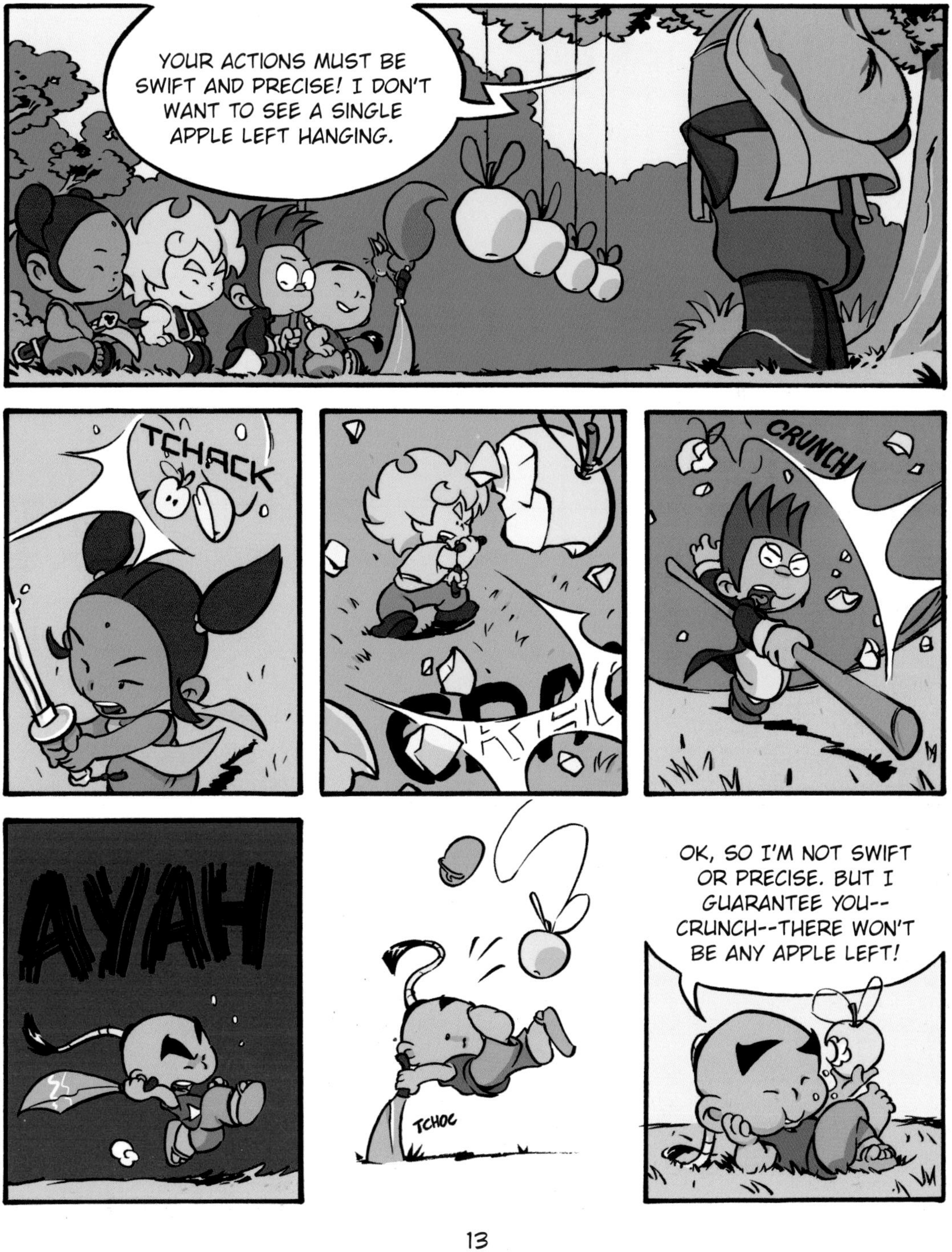

YOUR ACTIONS MUST BE SWIFT AND PRECISE! I DON'T WANT TO SEE A SINGLE APPLE LEFT HANGING.
TCHACK
CRUNCH
AYAH
TCHOC
OK, SO I'M NOT SWIFT OR PRECISE. BUT I GUARANTEE YOU--CRUNCH--THERE WON'T BE ANY APPLE LEFT!

Do unto Your Neighbor's Target

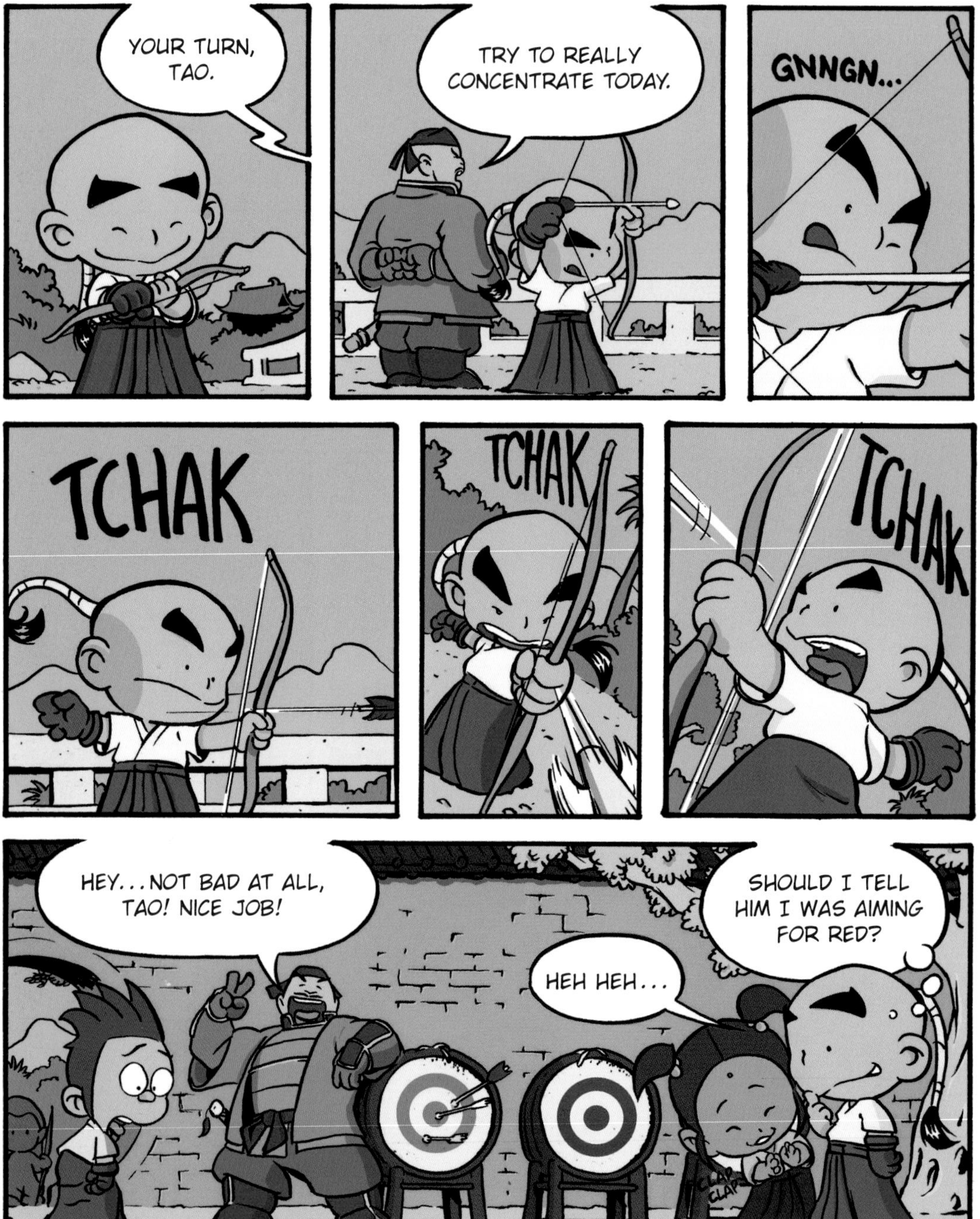
YOUR TURN, TAO.
TRY TO REALLY CONCENTRATE TODAY.
GNNGN...
TCHAK
TCHAK
TCHAK
HEY...NOT BAD AT ALL, TAO! NICE JOB!
HEH HEH...
SHOULD I TELL HIM I WAS AIMING FOR RED?

He Who Spies Gets a Black Eye

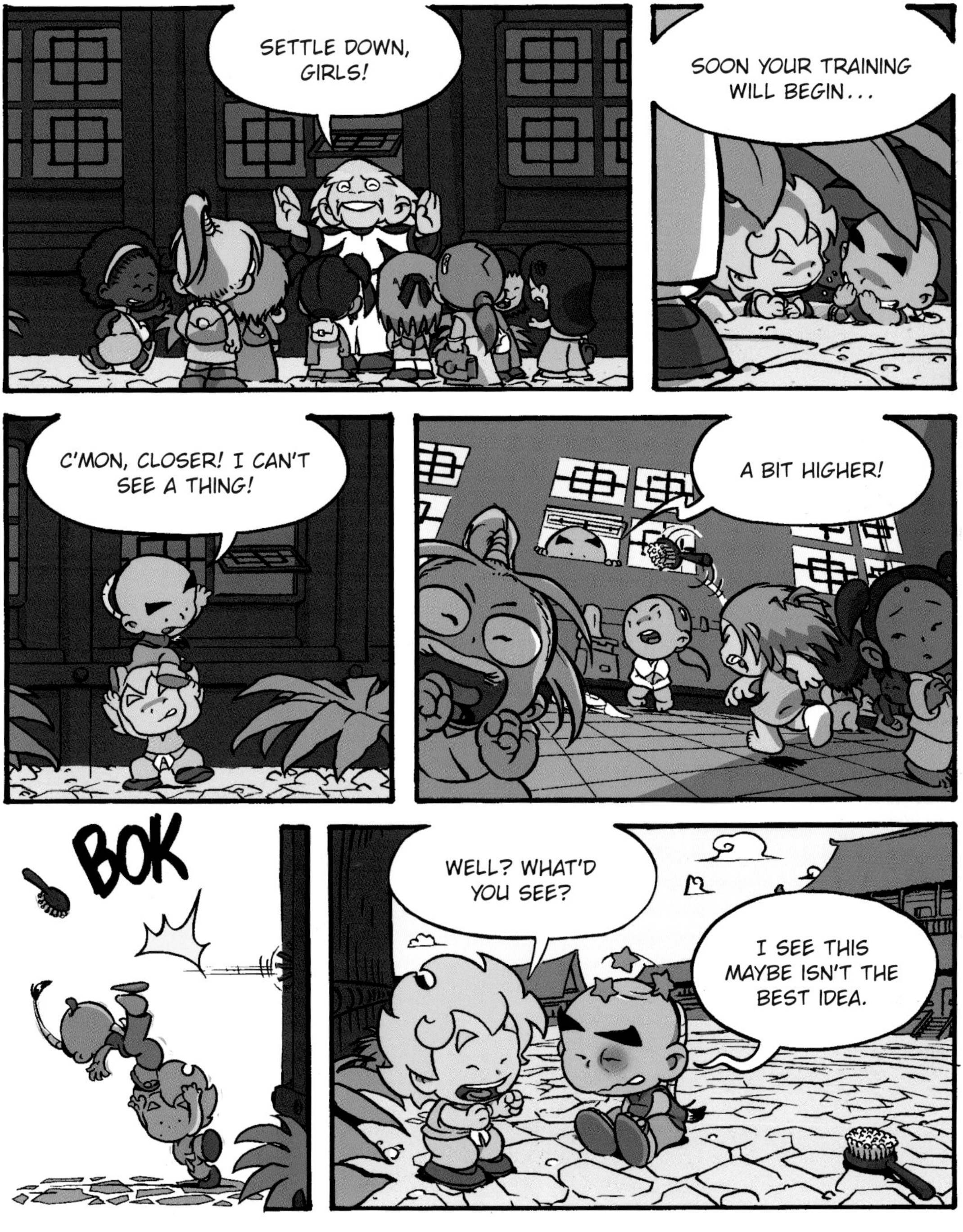
SETTLE DOWN, GIRLS!
SOON YOUR TRAINING WILL BEGIN...
C'MON, CLOSER! I CAN'T SEE A THING!
A BIT HIGHER!
BOK
WELL? WHAT'D YOU SEE?
I SEE THIS MAYBE ISN'T THE BEST IDEA.

The Enemy Within

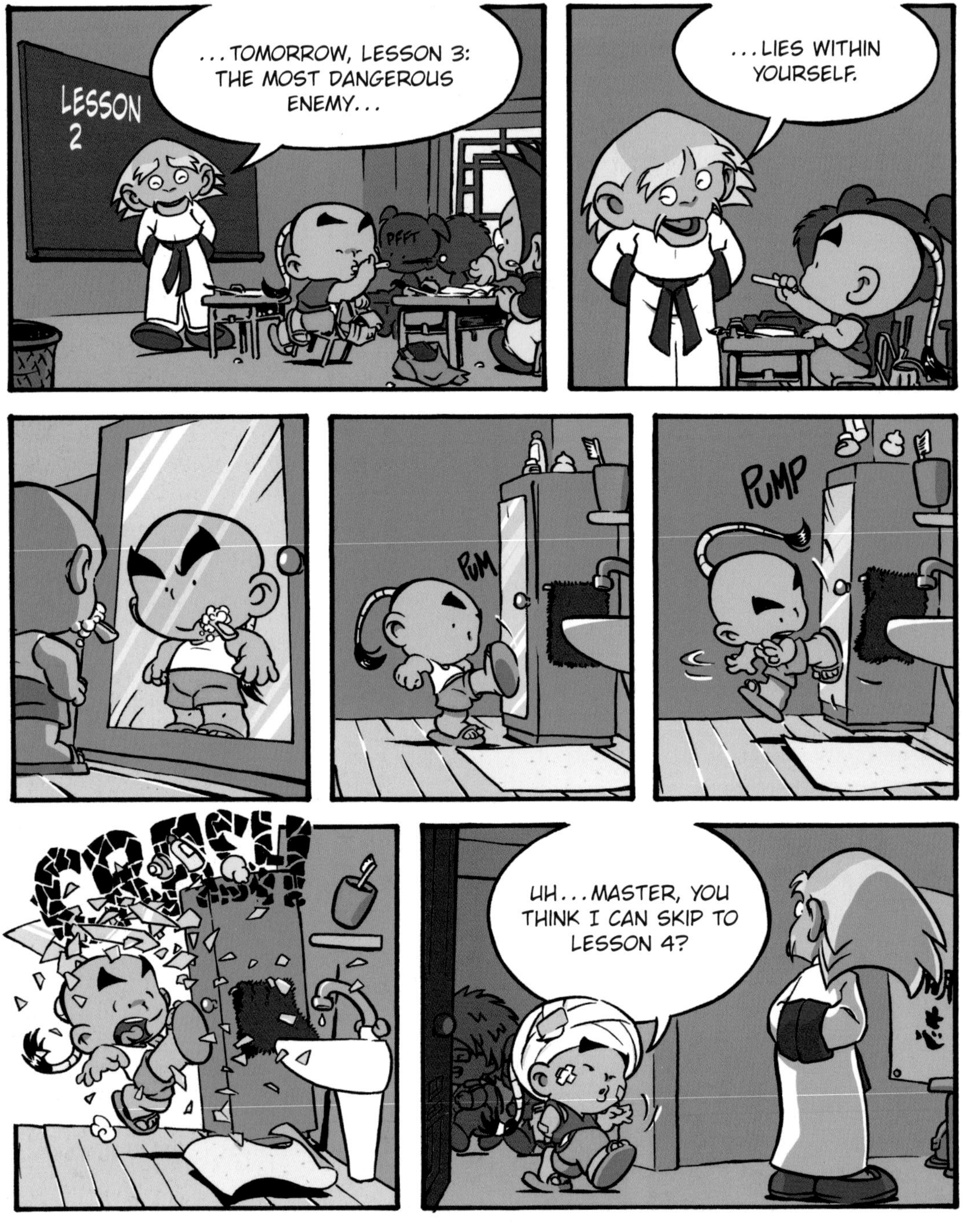
LESSON 2
...TOMORROW, LESSON 3: THE MOST DANGEROUS ENEMY...
PFFT
...LIES WITHIN YOURSELF.
PUM
PUMP
CRASH!
UH...MASTER, YOU THINK I CAN SKIP TO LESSON 4?

No Point Running If You're Going the Wrong Way

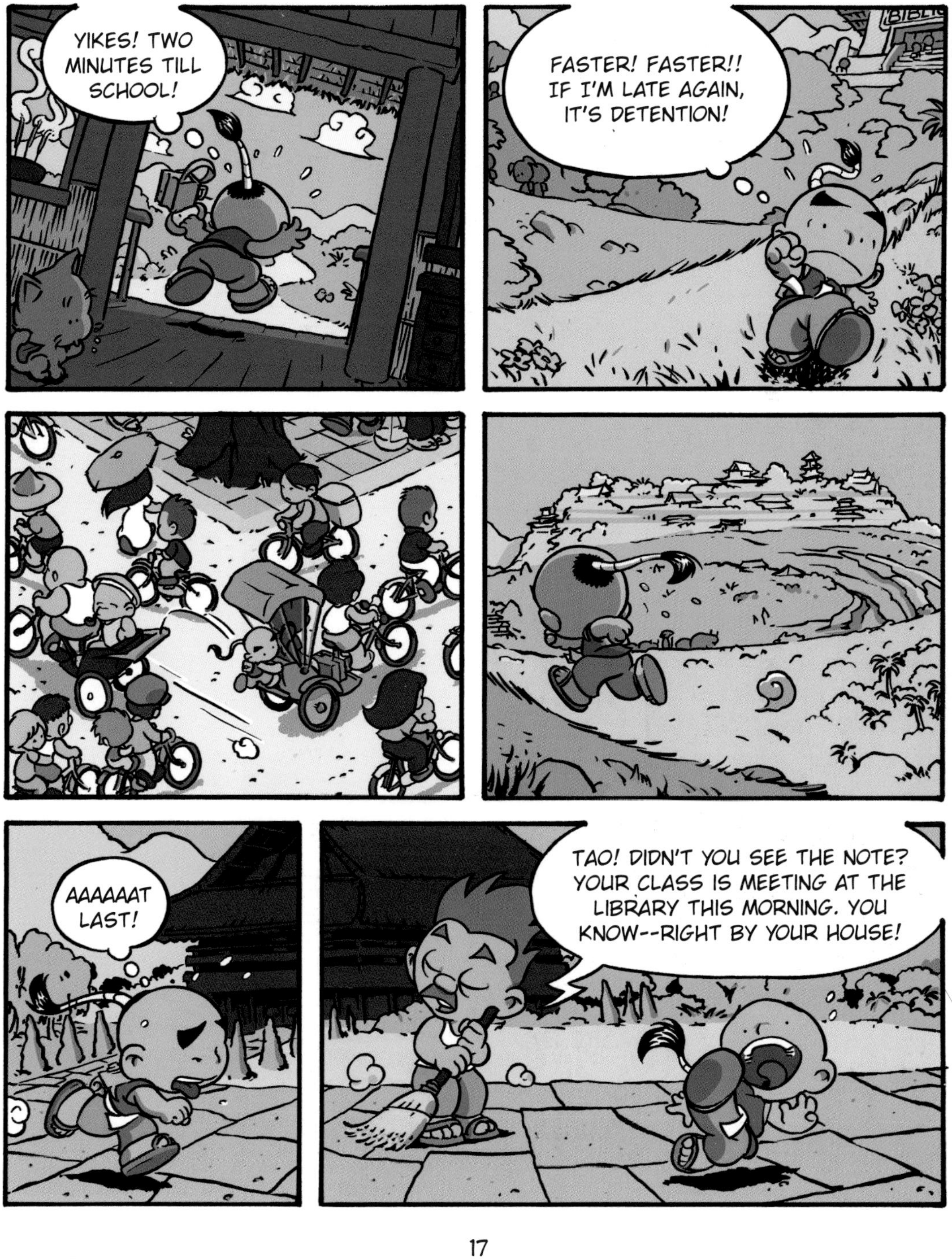

YIKES! TWO MINUTES TILL SCHOOL!
FASTER! FASTER!! IF I'M LATE AGAIN, IT'S DETENTION!
BIBLI
AAAAAAT LAST!
TAO! DIDN'T YOU SEE THE NOTE? YOUR CLASS IS MEETING AT THE LIBRARY THIS MORNING. YOU KNOW--RIGHT BY YOUR HOUSE!

Lessons within Lessons

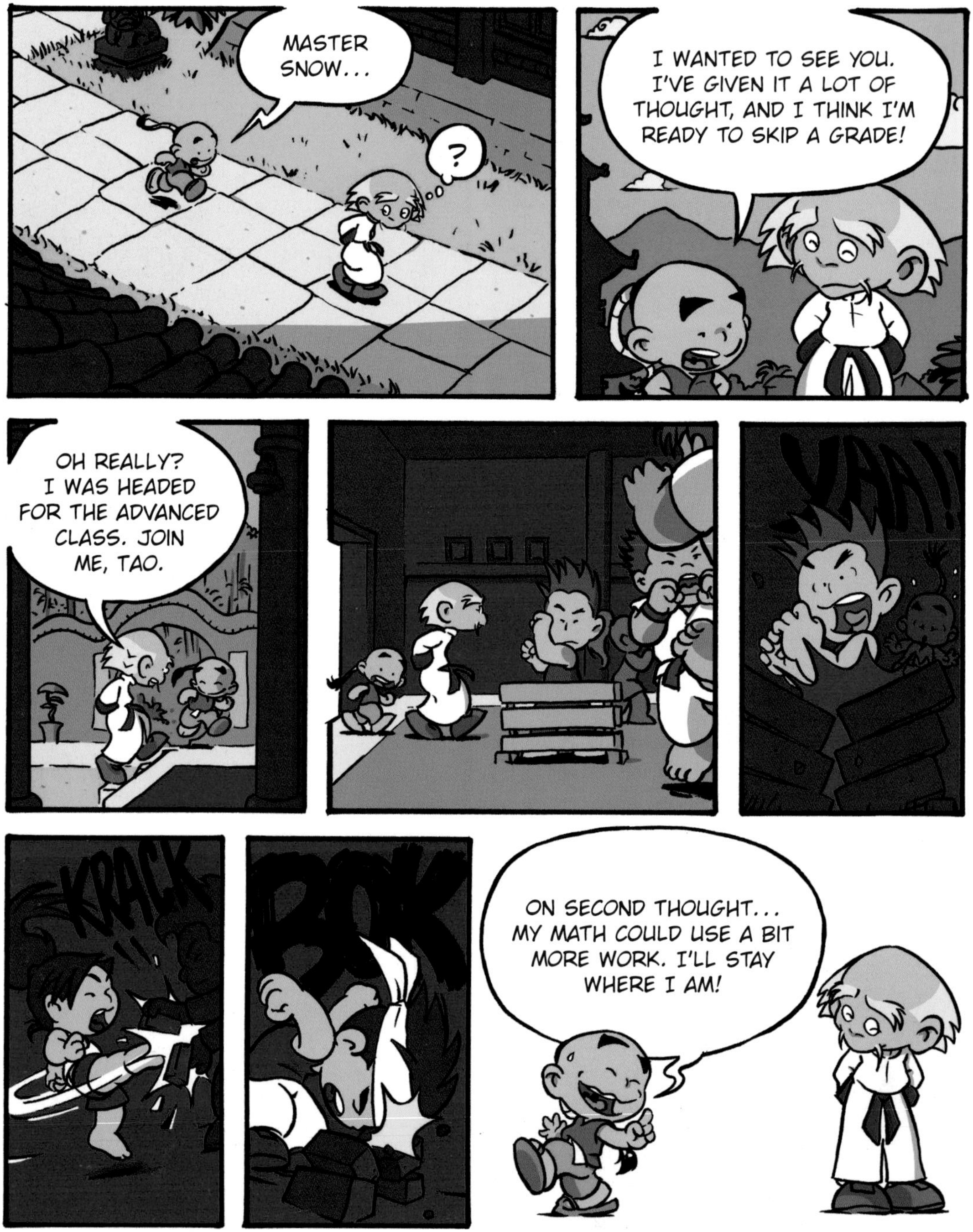
MASTER SNOW...
?
I WANTED TO SEE YOU. I'VE GIVEN IT A LOT OF THOUGHT, AND I THINK I'M READY TO SKIP A GRADE!
OH REALLY? I WAS HEADED FOR THE ADVANCED CLASS. JOIN ME, TAO.
YAH!!
KRACK
BOK
ON SECOND THOUGHT... MY MATH COULD USE A BIT MORE WORK. I'LL STAY WHERE I AM!

Long Is the Road That Leads to Lunch

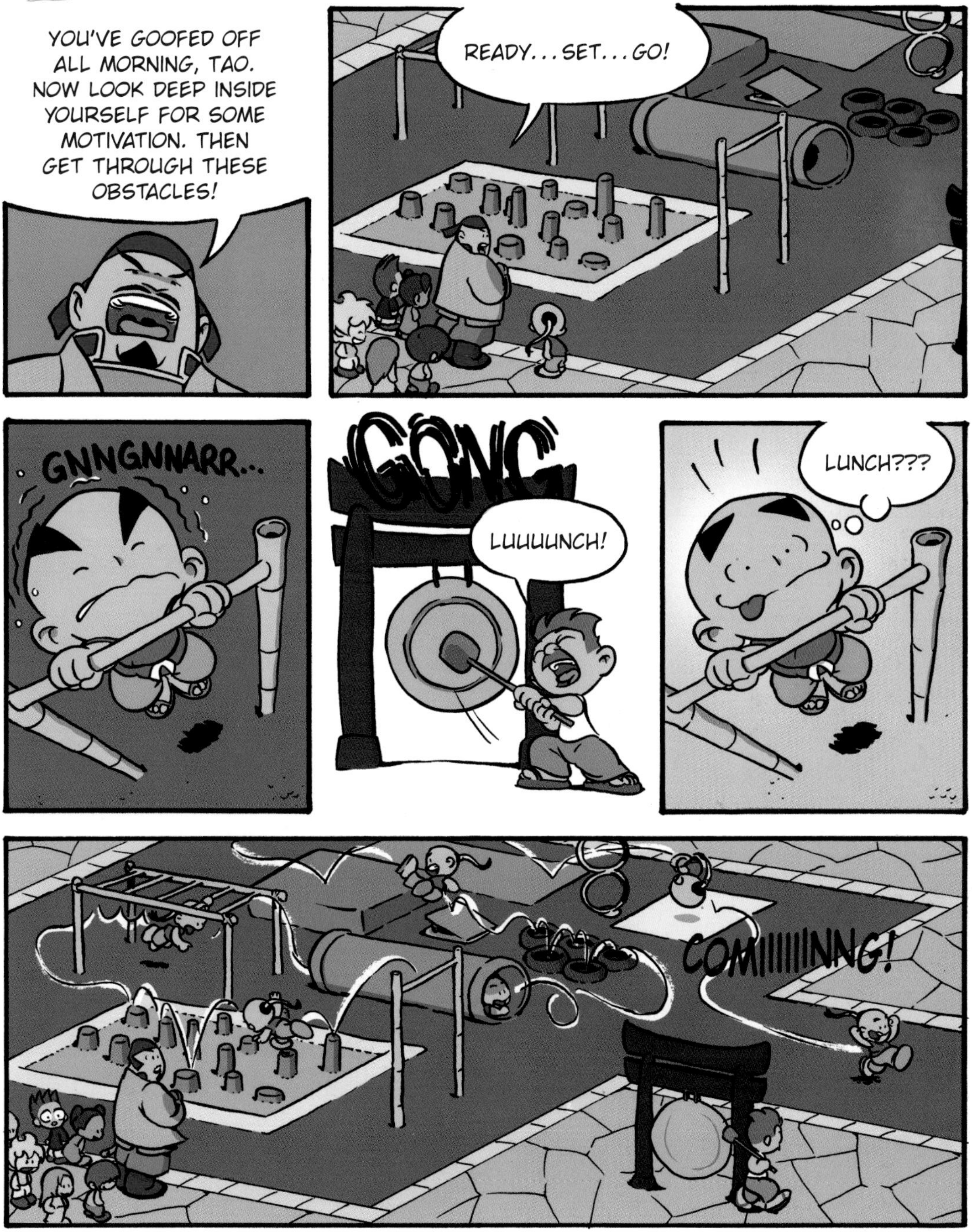
YOU'VE GOOFED OFF ALL MORNING, TAO. NOW LOOK DEEP INSIDE YOURSELF FOR SOME MOTIVATION. THEN GET THROUGH THESE OBSTACLES!
READY... SET... GO!
GNNGNNARR...
GONG
LUUUUNCH!
LUNCH???
COMIIIIIINNG!

The Joystick Is Mightier than the Sword

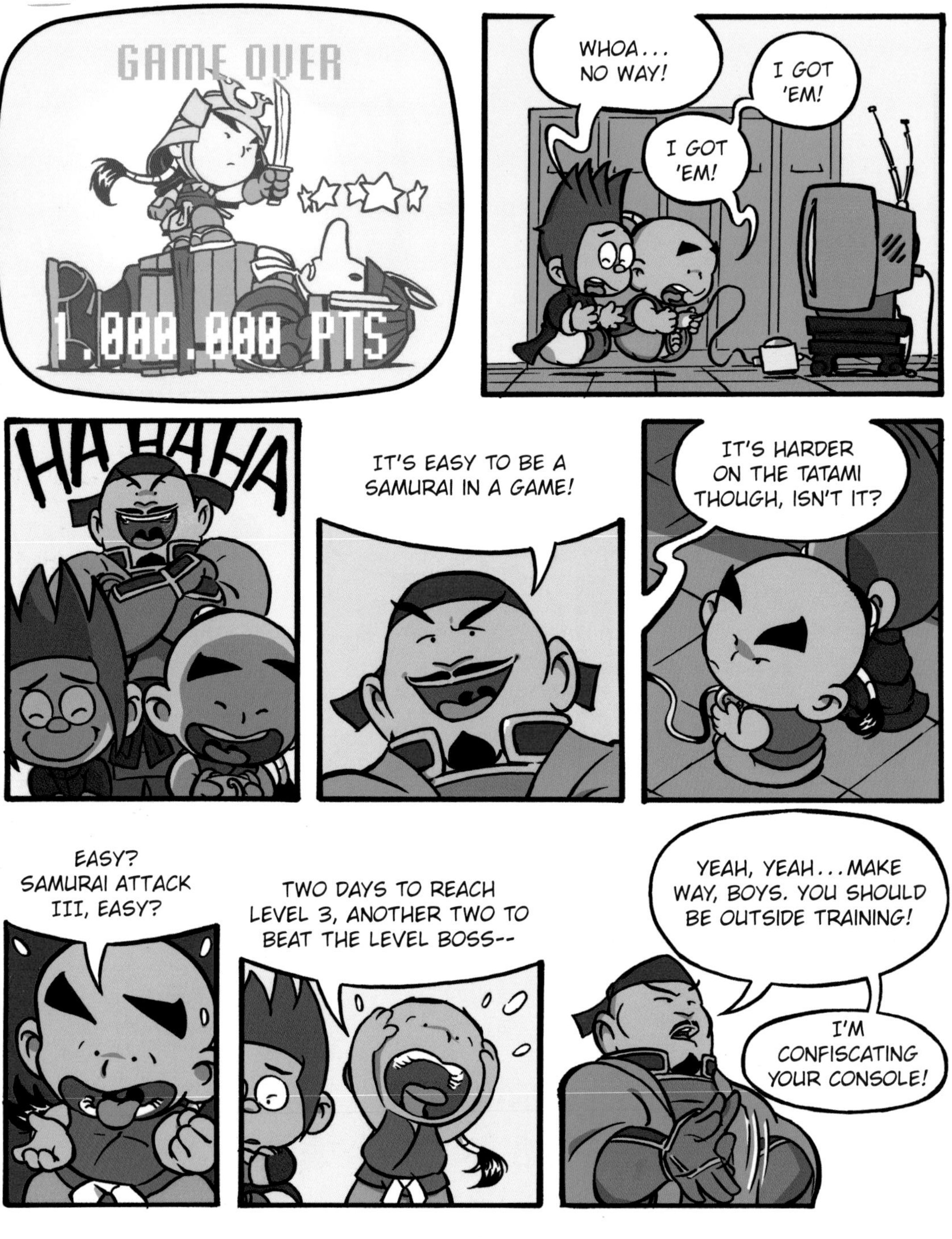
GAME OVER
1.000.000 PTS
WHOA... NO WAY!
I GOT 'EM!
I GOT 'EM!
HA HAHA
IT'S EASY TO BE A SAMURAI IN A GAME!
IT'S HARDER ON THE TATAMI THOUGH, ISN'T IT?
EASY? SAMURAI ATTACK III, EASY?
TWO DAYS TO REACH LEVEL 3, ANOTHER TWO TO BEAT THE LEVEL BOSS--
YEAH, YEAH... MAKE WAY, BOYS. YOU SHOULD BE OUTSIDE TRAINING!
I'M CONFISCATING YOUR CONSOLE!

The Next Day...

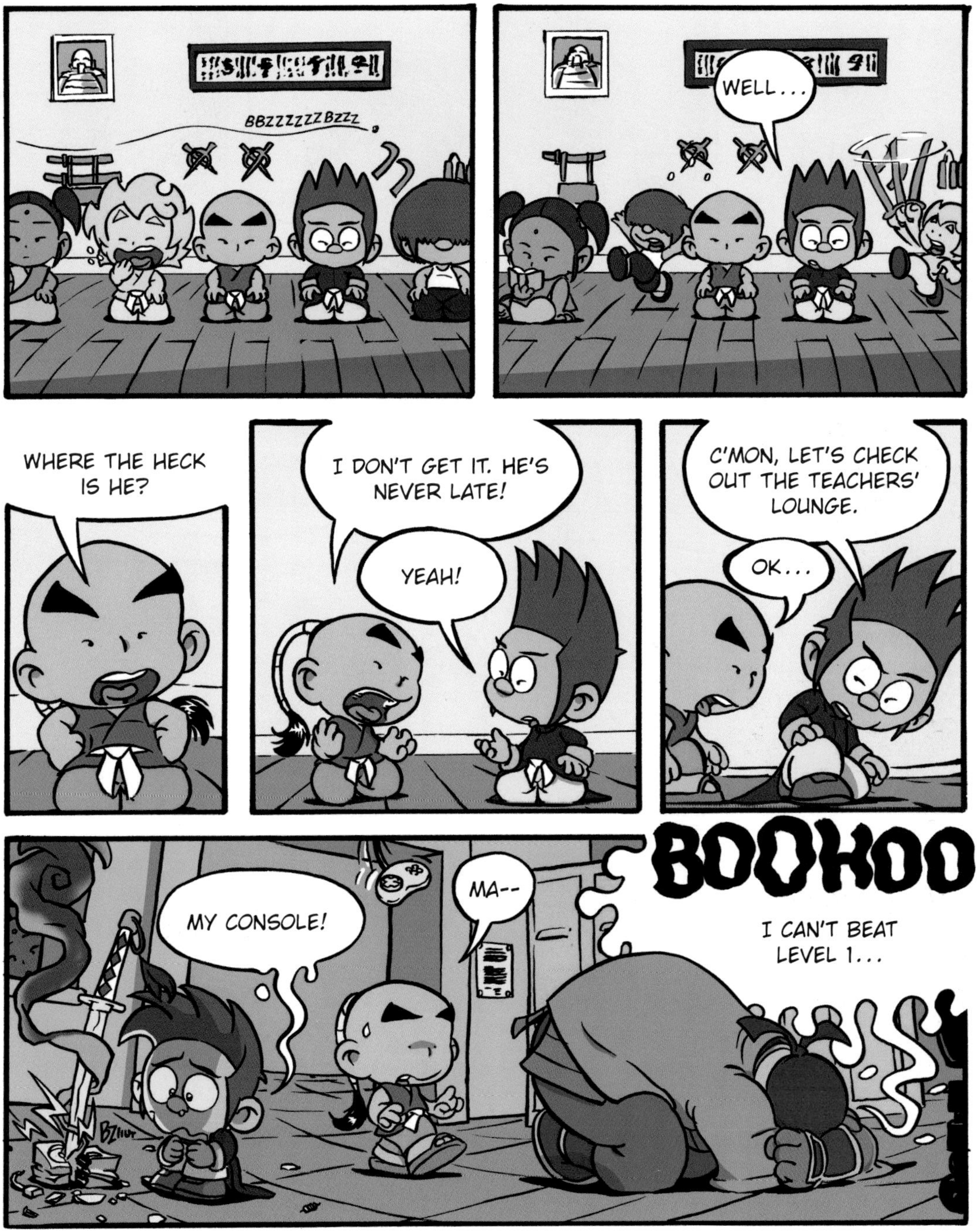
BBZZZZZZBZZZ
WELL...
WHERE THE HECK IS HE?
I DON'T GET IT. HE'S NEVER LATE!
YEAH!
C'MON, LET'S CHECK OUT THE TEACHERS' LOUNGE.
OK...
MY CONSOLE!
MA--
BOOHOO
I CAN'T BEAT LEVEL 1...

Wise Men Waste No Words

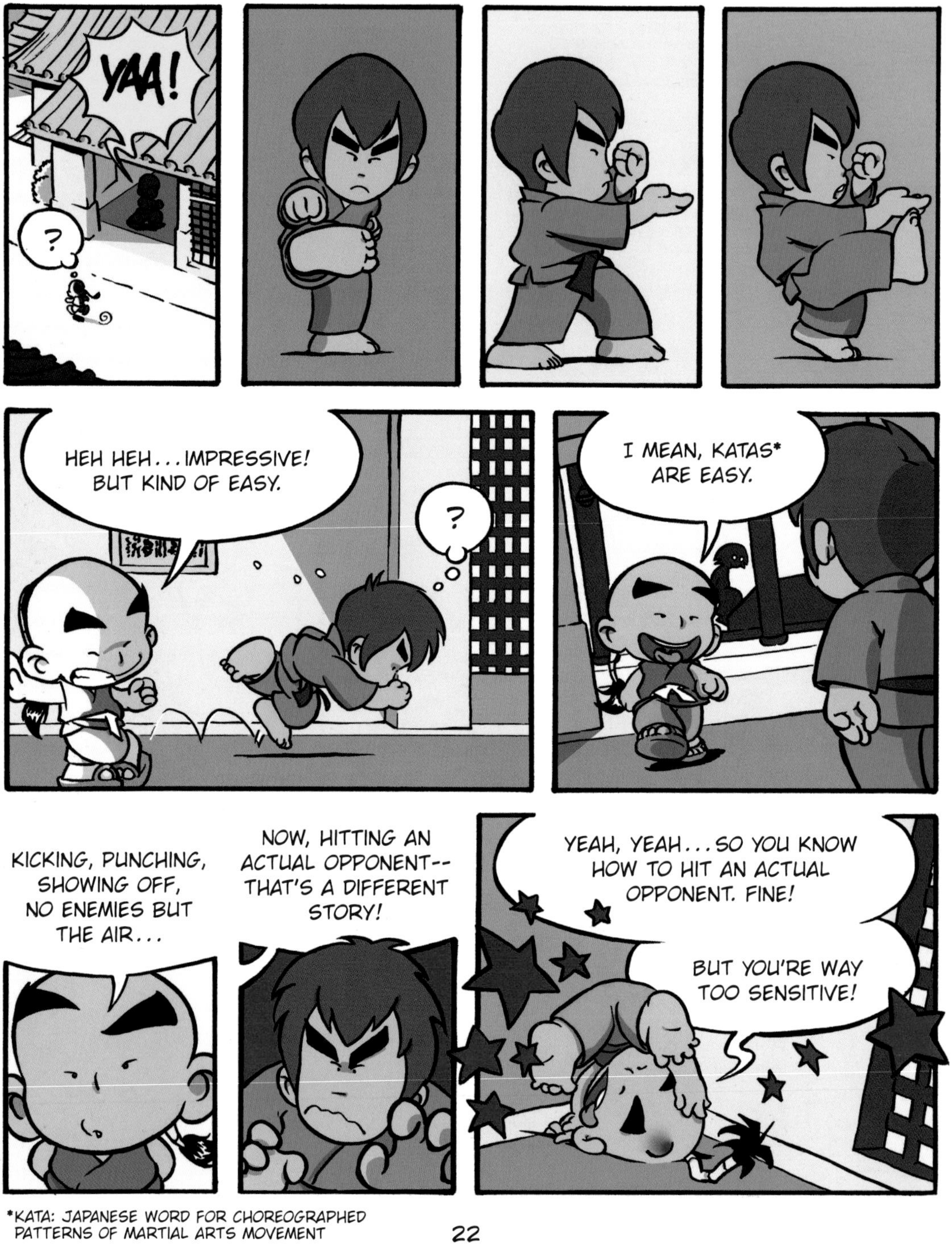
YAA!
?
HEH HEH...IMPRESSIVE! BUT KIND OF EASY.
?
I MEAN, KATAS* ARE EASY.
KICKING, PUNCHING, SHOWING OFF, NO ENEMIES BUT THE AIR...
NOW, HITTING AN ACTUAL OPPONENT--THAT'S A DIFFERENT STORY!
YEAH, YEAH...SO YOU KNOW HOW TO HIT AN ACTUAL OPPONENT. FINE!
BUT YOU'RE WAY TOO SENSITIVE!

*KATA: JAPANESE WORD FOR CHOREOGRAPHED PATTERNS OF MARTIAL ARTS MOVEMENT

A Chirping Grasshopper Makes for Noisy Silence

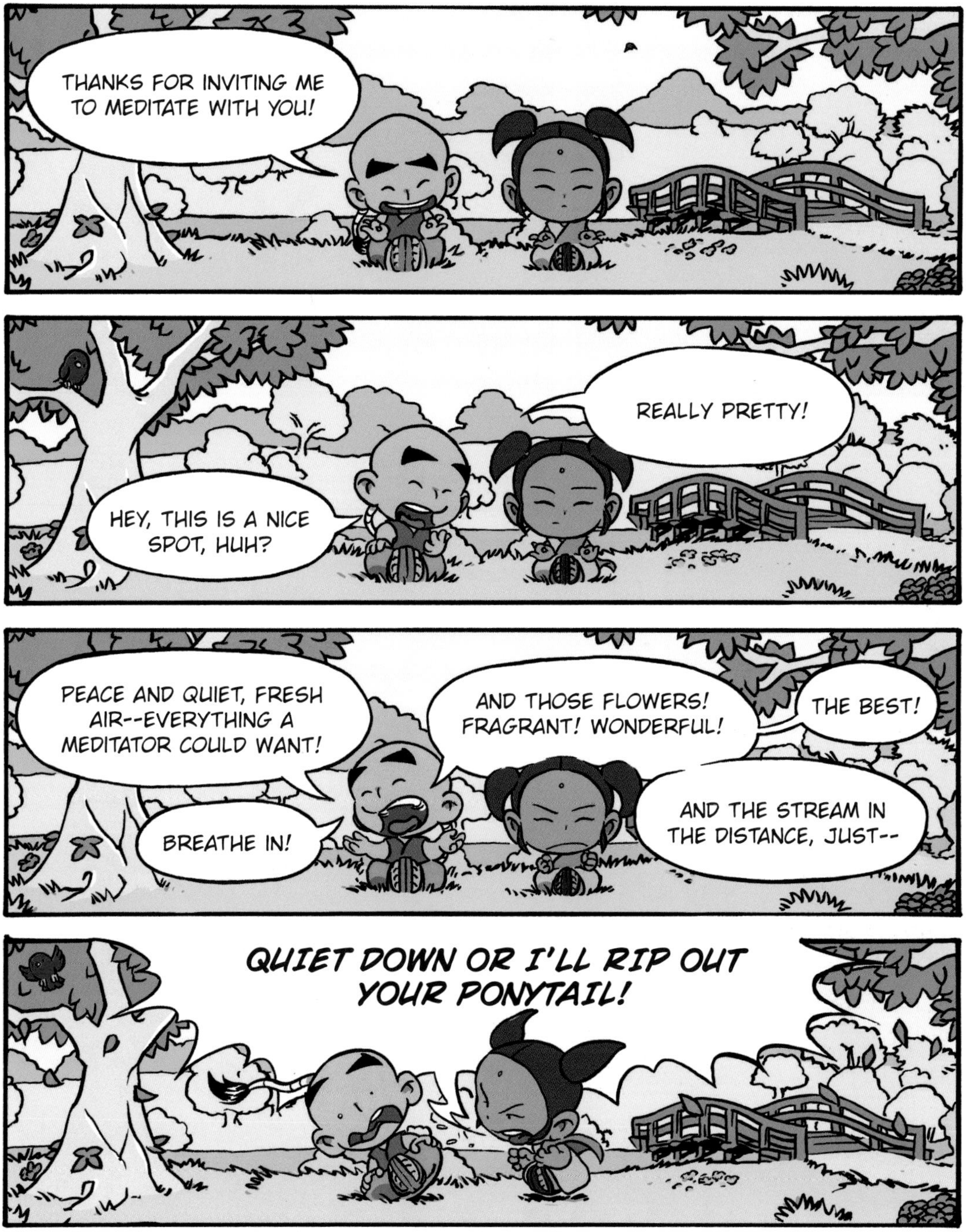

THANKS FOR INVITING ME TO MEDITATE WITH YOU!
HEY, THIS IS A NICE SPOT, HUH?
REALLY PRETTY!
PEACE AND QUIET, FRESH AIR--EVERYTHING A MEDITATOR COULD WANT!
BREATHE IN!
AND THOSE FLOWERS! FRAGRANT! WONDERFUL!
THE BEST!
AND THE STREAM IN THE DISTANCE, JUST--
QUIET DOWN OR I'LL RIP OUT YOUR PONYTAIL!

Reading Can Prevent Kata-strophe

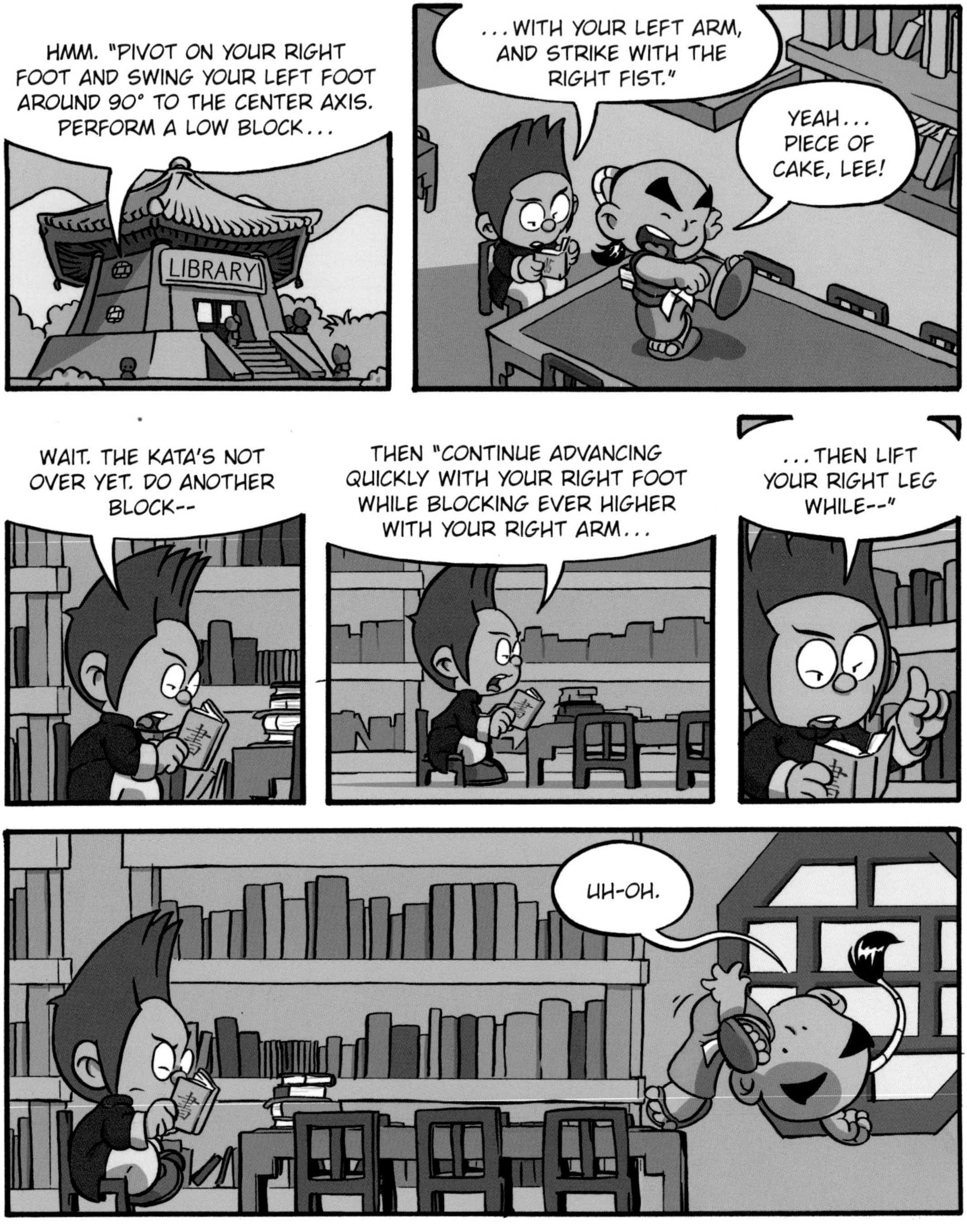
HMM. "PIVOT ON YOUR RIGHT FOOT AND SWING YOUR LEFT FOOT AROUND 90° TO THE CENTER AXIS. PERFORM A LOW BLOCK...
LIBRARY
...WITH YOUR LEFT ARM, AND STRIKE WITH THE RIGHT FIST."
YEAH... PIECE OF CAKE, LEE!
WAIT. THE KATA'S NOT OVER YET. DO ANOTHER BLOCK--
THEN "CONTINUE ADVANCING QUICKLY WITH YOUR RIGHT FOOT WHILE BLOCKING EVER HIGHER WITH YOUR RIGHT ARM...
...THEN LIFT YOUR RIGHT LEG WHILE--"
UH-OH.

The Great Dragon Eats the Tiny Boat

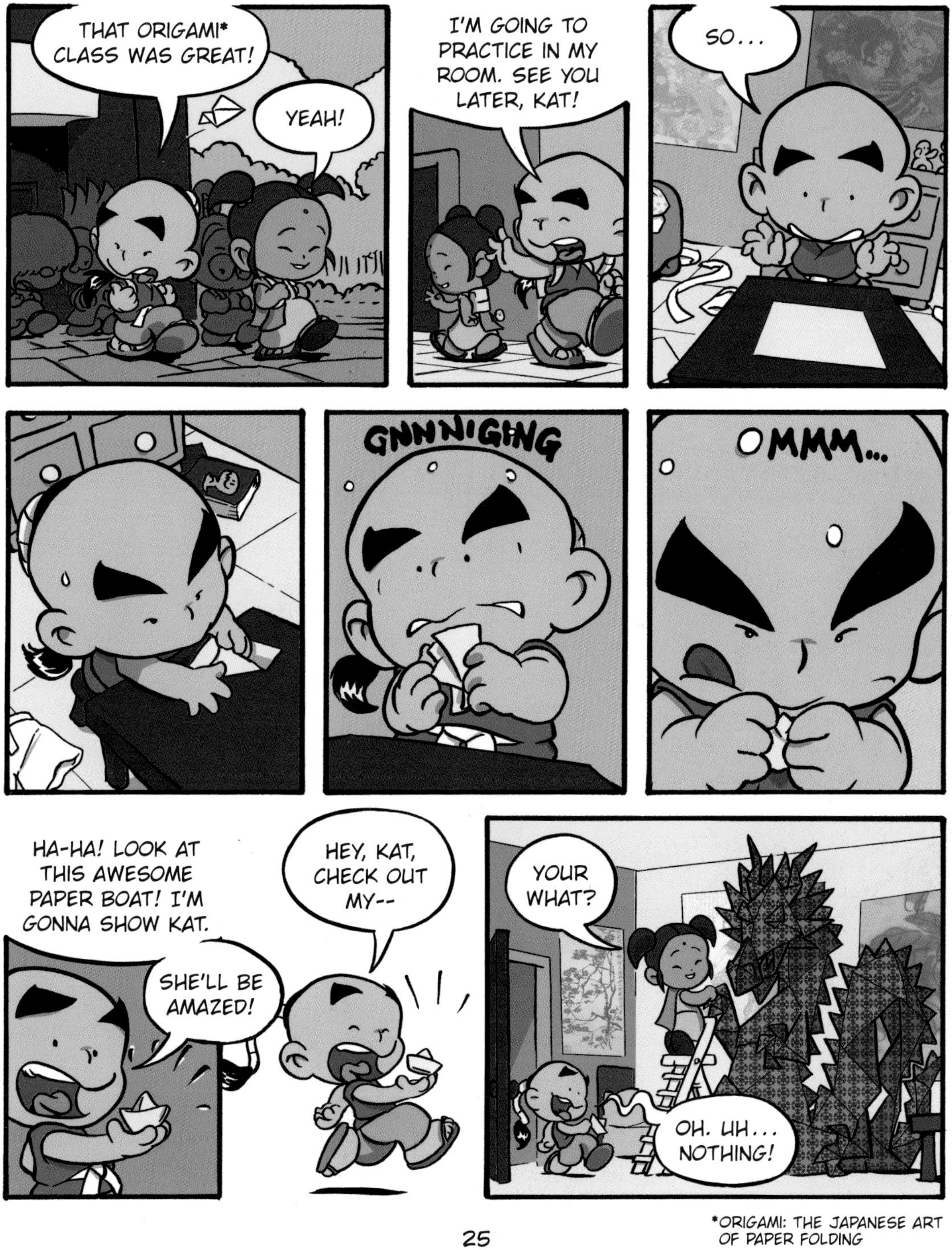
THAT ORIGAMI* CLASS WAS GREAT!
YEAH!
I'M GOING TO PRACTICE IN MY ROOM. SEE YOU LATER, KAT!
SO...
GNNNIGING
OMMM...
HA-HA! LOOK AT THIS AWESOME PAPER BOAT! I'M GONNA SHOW KAT.
SHE'LL BE AMAZED!
HEY, KAT, CHECK OUT MY--
YOUR WHAT?
OH. UH... NOTHING!

*ORIGAMI: THE JAPANESE ART OF PAPER FOLDING

Soul of a Poet, Belly of a Hungry Man

BEAUTIFUL.
HOW PEACEFUL!
THOSE COLORS, THE SWEEPING LINES, THE SNOWCAPPED PEAK!
PURE POETRY! IT BRINGS A TEAR TO MY EYE.
WHEN DO WE EAT?
IT LOOKS LIKE A HUGE CREAM PUFF!
TAO, YOU'RE REALLY HOPELESS.

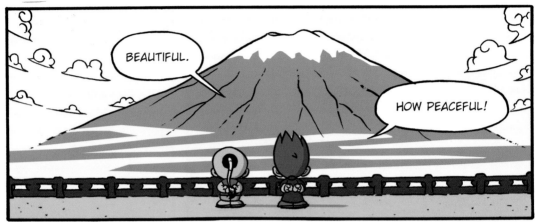

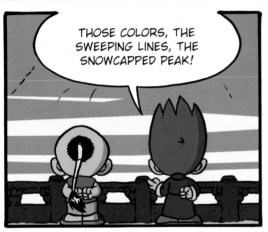

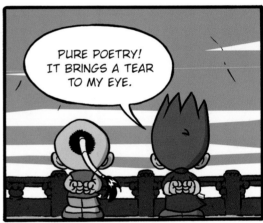

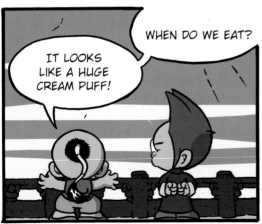

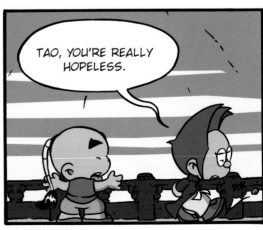

The Horror, the Horror

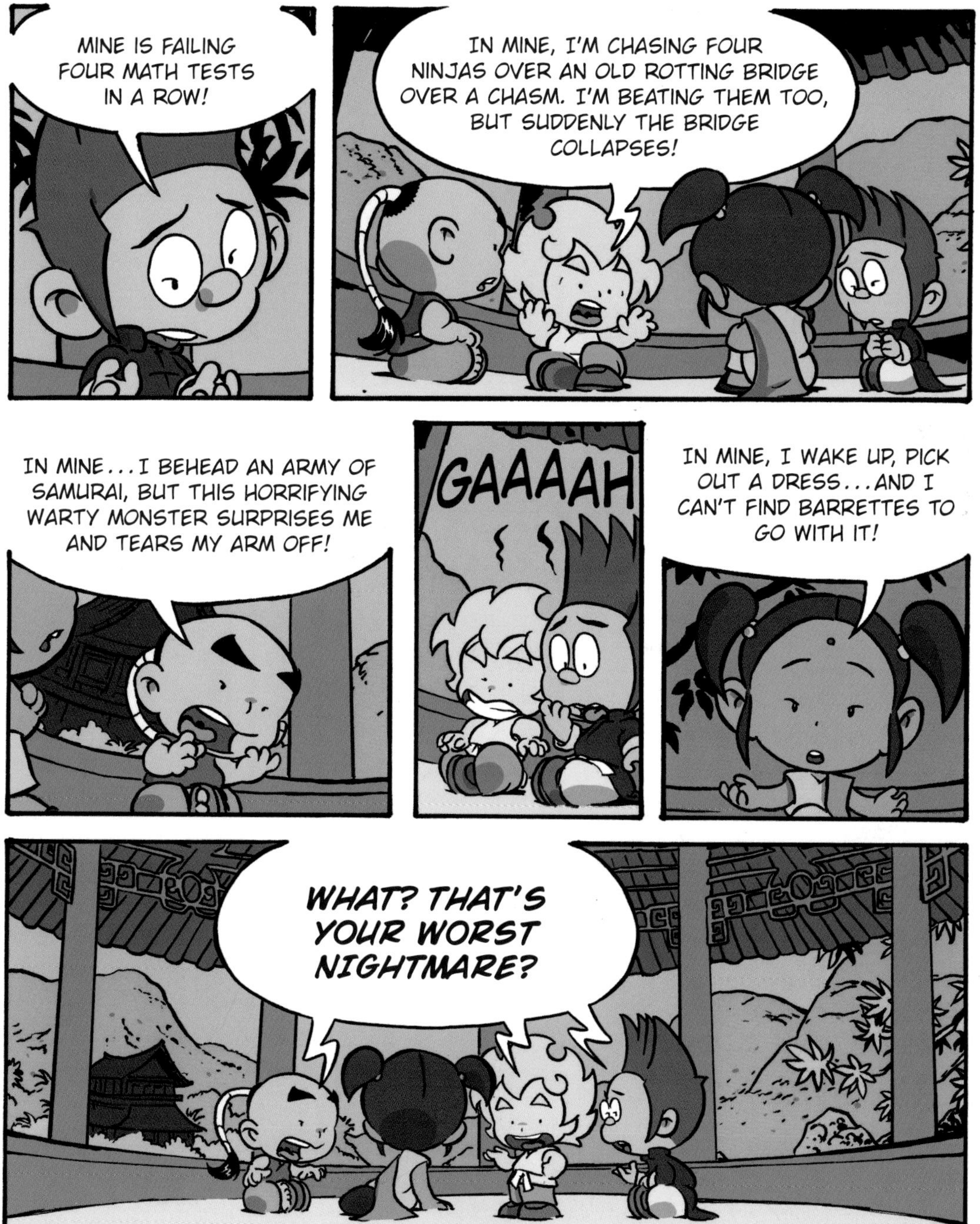
MINE IS FAILING FOUR MATH TESTS IN A ROW!
IN MINE, I'M CHASING FOUR NINJAS OVER AN OLD ROTTING BRIDGE OVER A CHASM. I'M BEATING THEM TOO, BUT SUDDENLY THE BRIDGE COLLAPSES!
IN MINE . . . I BEHEAD AN ARMY OF SAMURAI, BUT THIS HORRIFYING WARTY MONSTER SURPRISES ME AND TEARS MY ARM OFF!
GAAAAH
IN MINE, I WAKE UP, PICK OUT A DRESS . . . AND I CAN'T FIND BARRETTES TO GO WITH IT!
WHAT? THAT'S YOUR WORST NIGHTMARE?

Good, Clean Fun

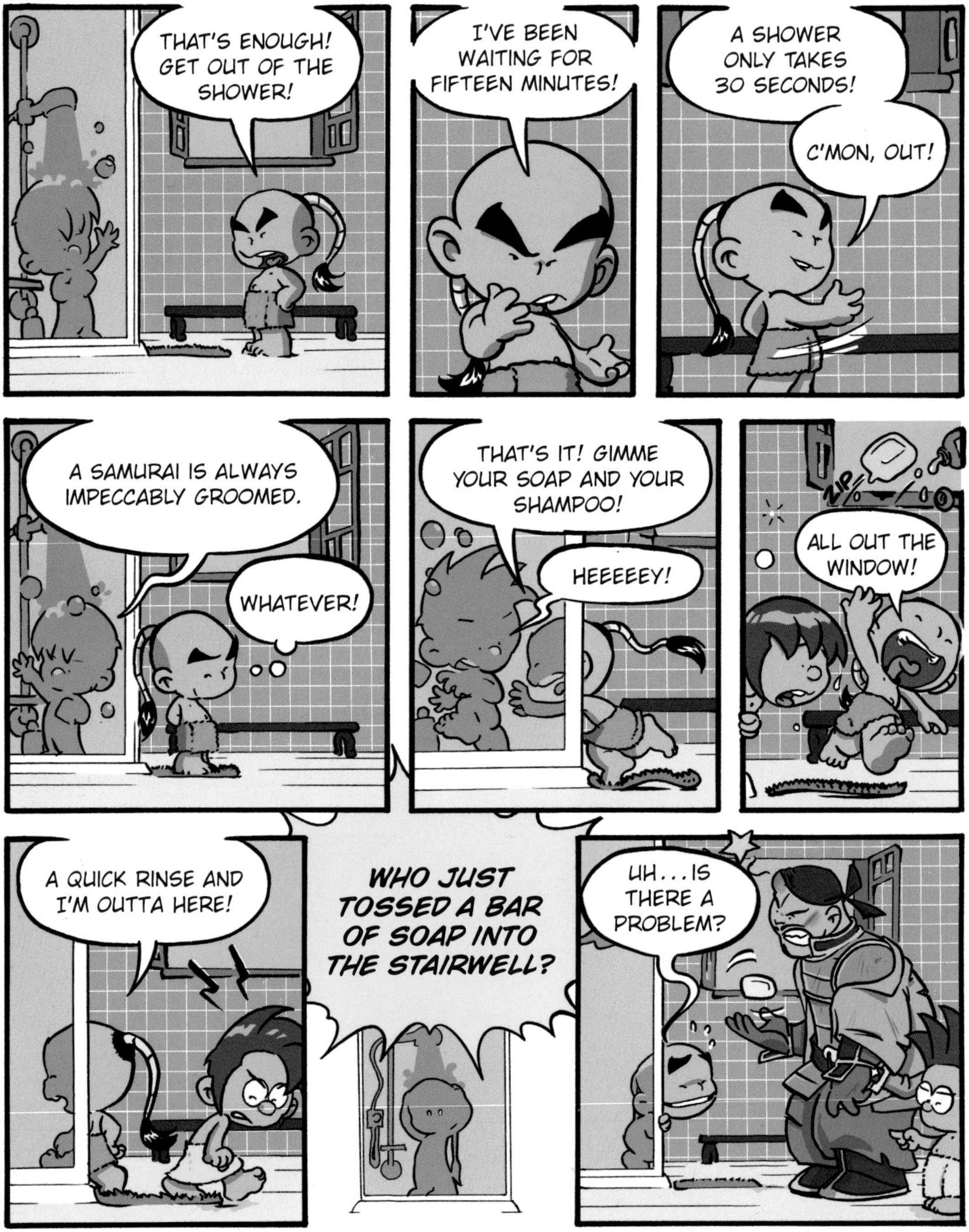

THAT'S ENOUGH! GET OUT OF THE SHOWER!
I'VE BEEN WAITING FOR FIFTEEN MINUTES!
A SHOWER ONLY TAKES 30 SECONDS!
C'MON, OUT!
A SAMURAI IS ALWAYS IMPECCABLY GROOMED.
WHATEVER!
THAT'S IT! GIMME YOUR SOAP AND YOUR SHAMPOO!
HEEEEEY!
ZIP
ALL OUT THE WINDOW!
A QUICK RINSE AND I'M OUTTA HERE!
WHO JUST TOSSED A BAR OF SOAP INTO THE STAIRWELL?
UH . . . IS THERE A PROBLEM?

Low-Down, Dirty Thieves

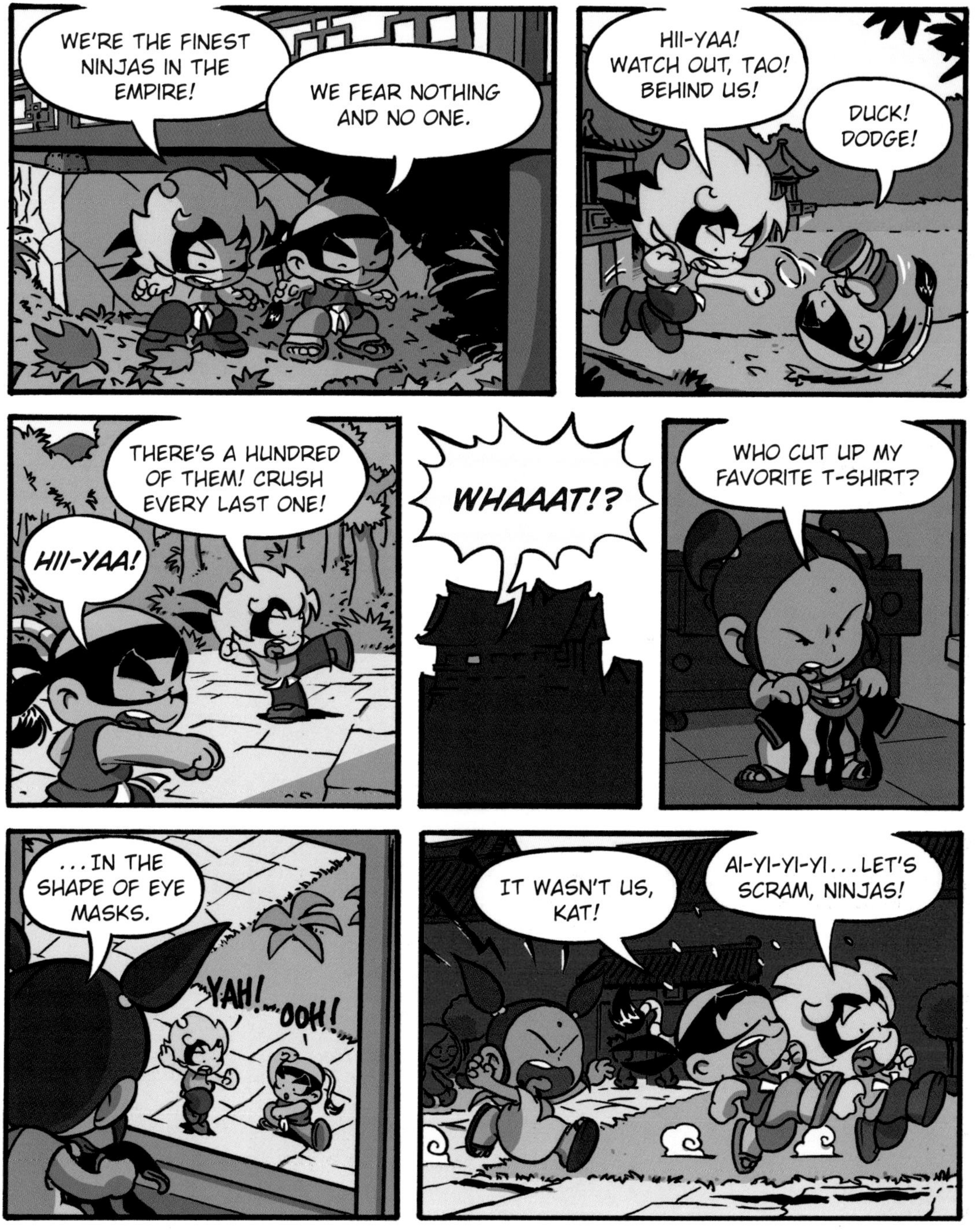

WE'RE THE FINEST NINJAS IN THE EMPIRE!
WE FEAR NOTHING AND NO ONE.
HII-YAA! WATCH OUT, TAO! BEHIND US!
DUCK! DODGE!
THERE'S A HUNDRED OF THEM! CRUSH EVERY LAST ONE!
HII-YAA!
WHAAAT!?
WHO CUT UP MY FAVORITE T-SHIRT?
...IN THE SHAPE OF EYE MASKS.
YAH!
OOH!
IT WASN'T US, KAT!
AI-YI-YI-YI...LET'S SCRAM, NINJAS!

The Prideful Peacock Speaks Too Soon

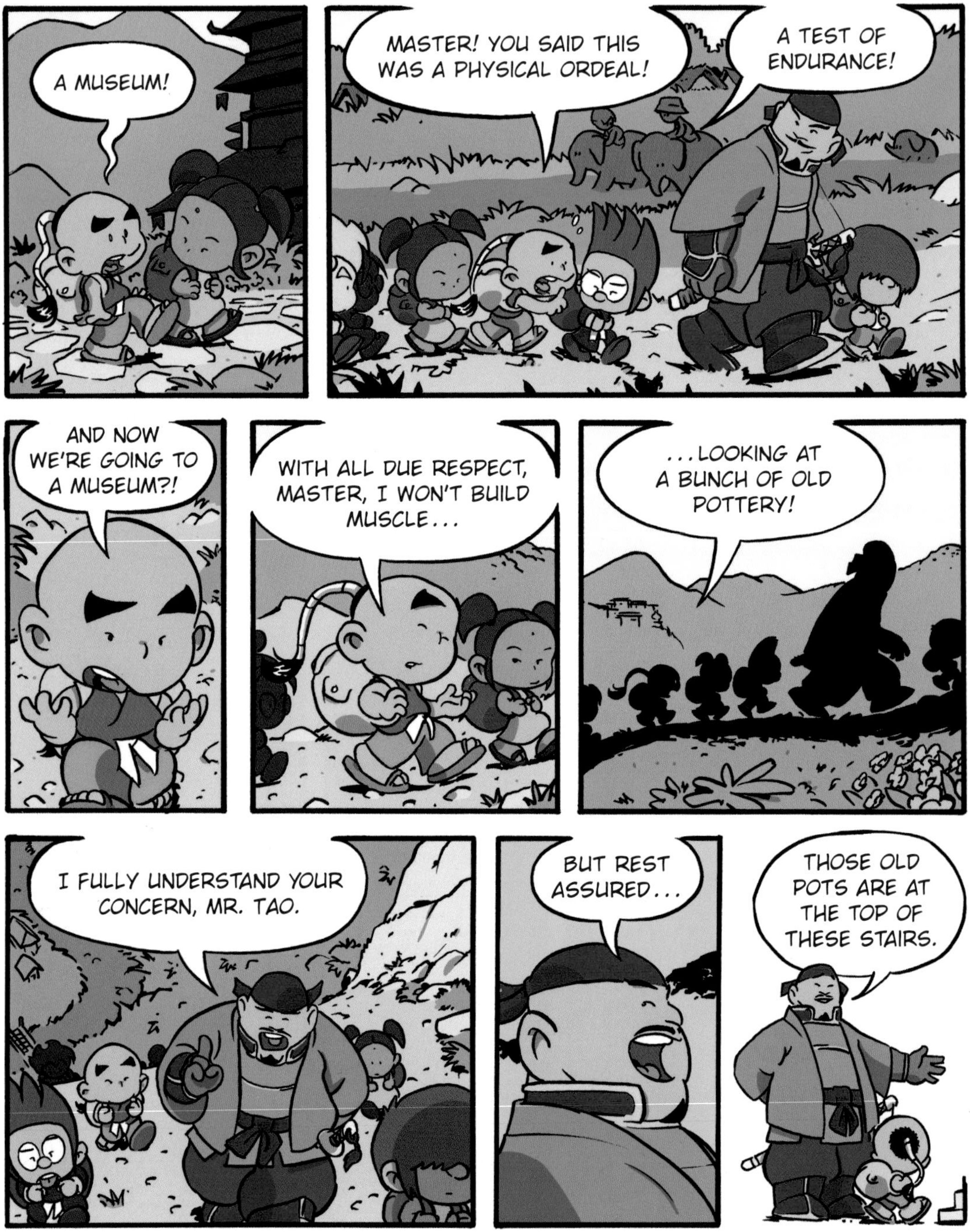
A MUSEUM!
MASTER! YOU SAID THIS WAS A PHYSICAL ORDEAL!
A TEST OF ENDURANCE!
AND NOW WE'RE GOING TO A MUSEUM?!
WITH ALL DUE RESPECT, MASTER, I WON'T BUILD MUSCLE...
...LOOKING AT A BUNCH OF OLD POTTERY!
I FULLY UNDERSTAND YOUR CONCERN, MR. TAO.
BUT REST ASSURED...
THOSE OLD POTS ARE AT THE TOP OF THESE STAIRS.

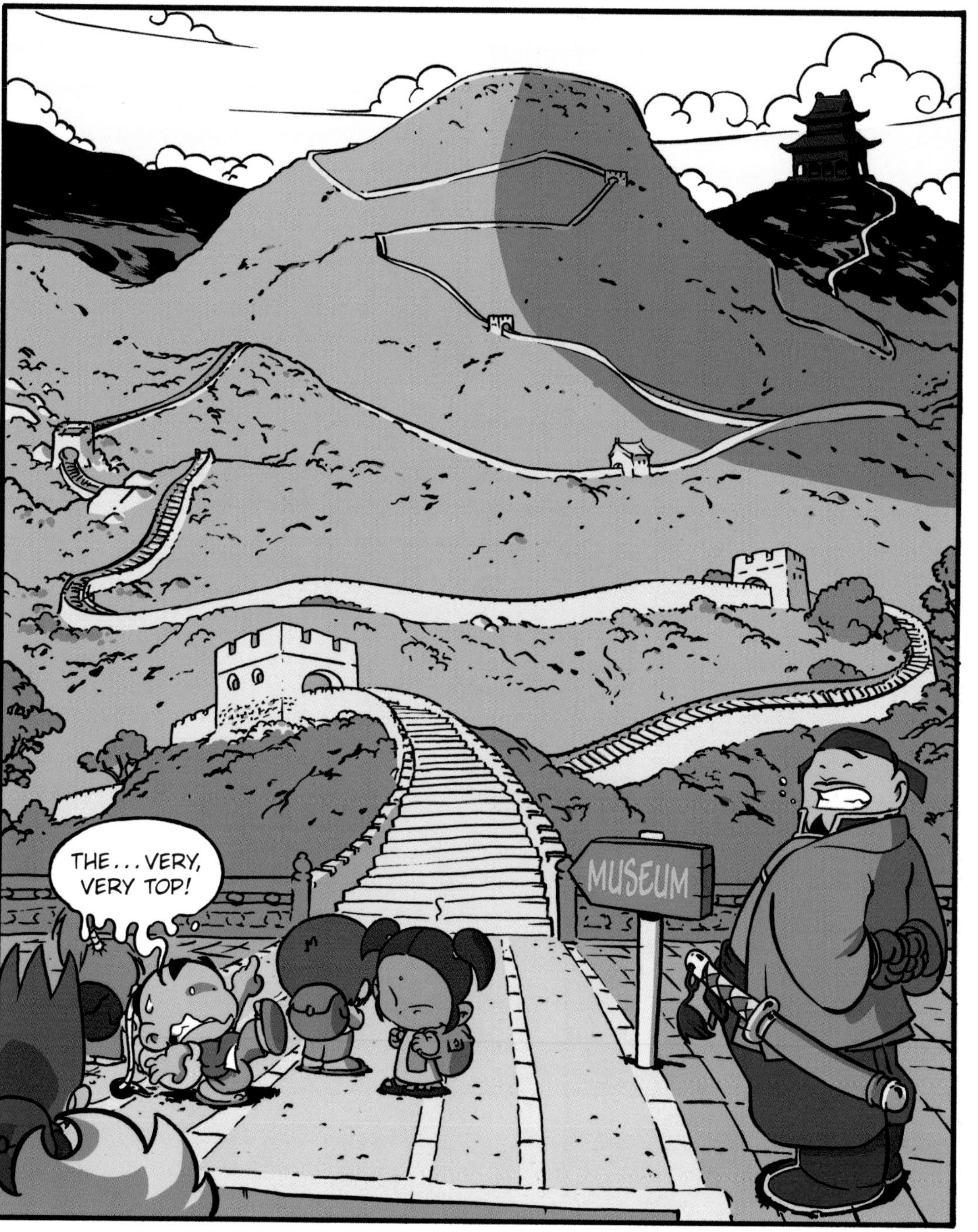
THE... VERY, VERY TOP!
MUSEUM

Choose Your Opponents Wisely

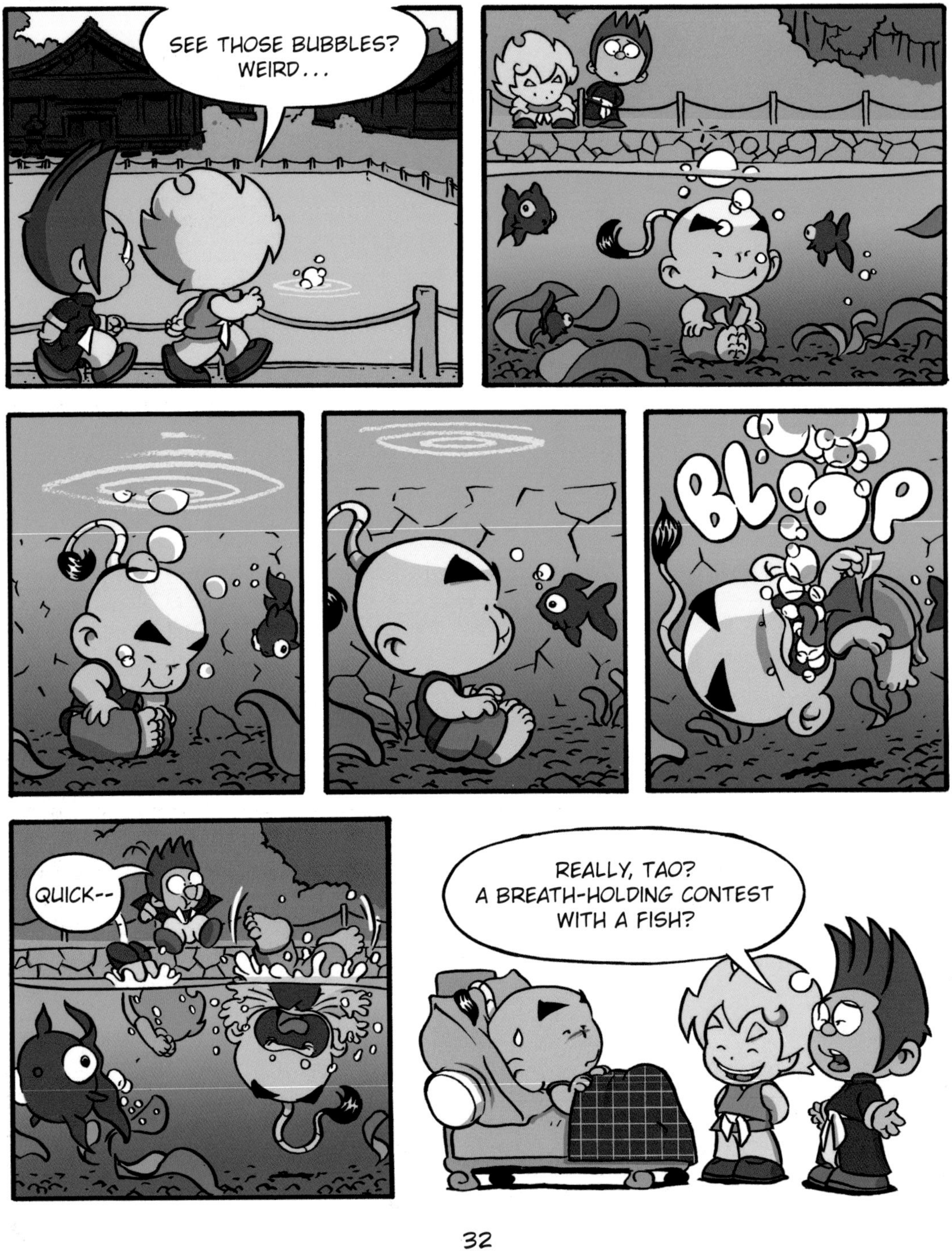

SEE THOSE BUBBLES? WEIRD...
BLOOP
QUICK--
REALLY, TAO? A BREATH-HOLDING CONTEST WITH A FISH?

One Monster May Hide Another

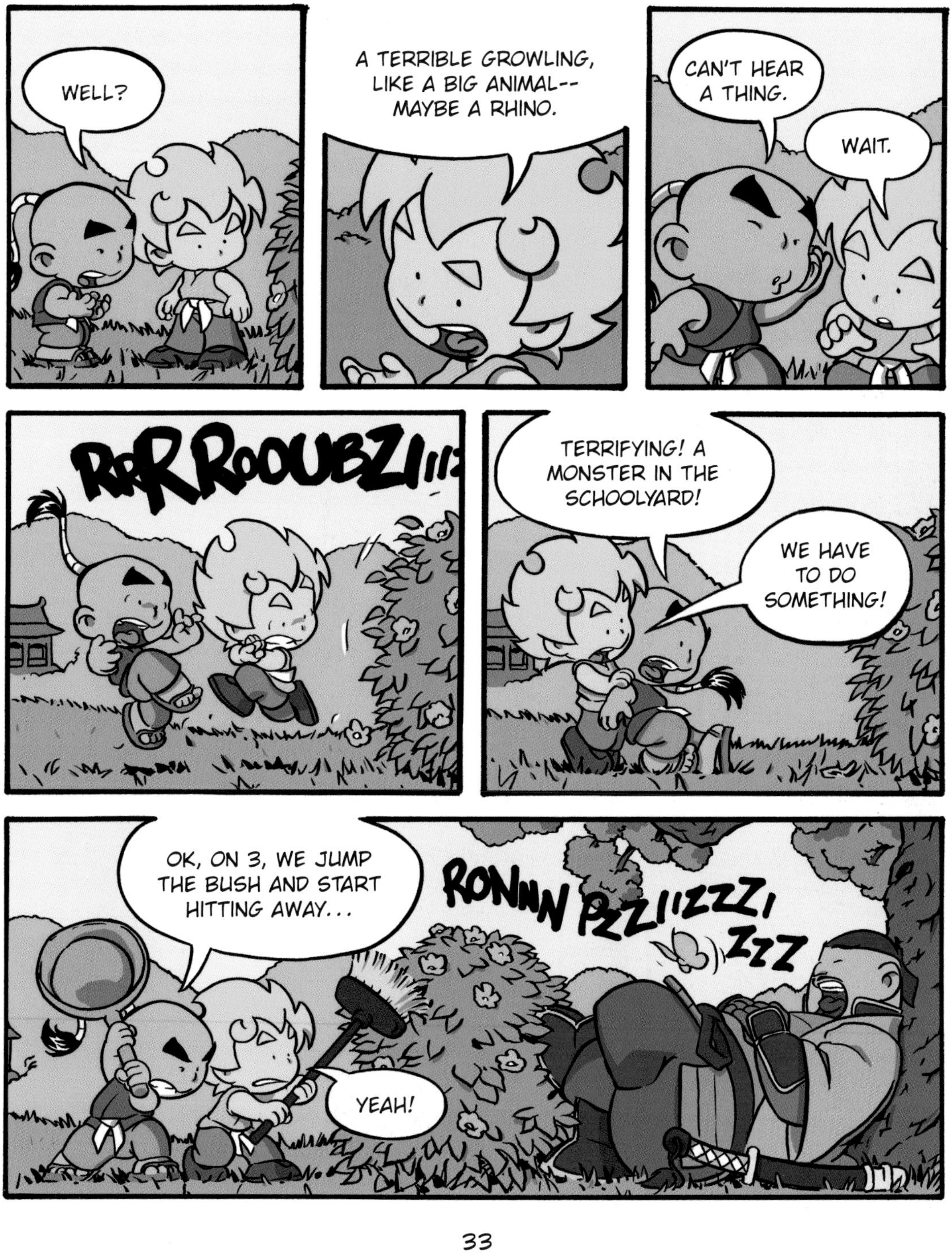
WELL?
A TERRIBLE GROWLING, LIKE A BIG ANIMAL-- MAYBE A RHINO.
CAN'T HEAR A THING.
WAIT.
RRRROOUBZI!!
TERRIFYING! A MONSTER IN THE SCHOOLYARD!
WE HAVE TO DO SOMETHING!
OK, ON 3, WE JUMP THE BUSH AND START HITTING AWAY...
RONNN PZZI!ZZZI ZZZ
YEAH!

A Grandmaster Has His Secrets

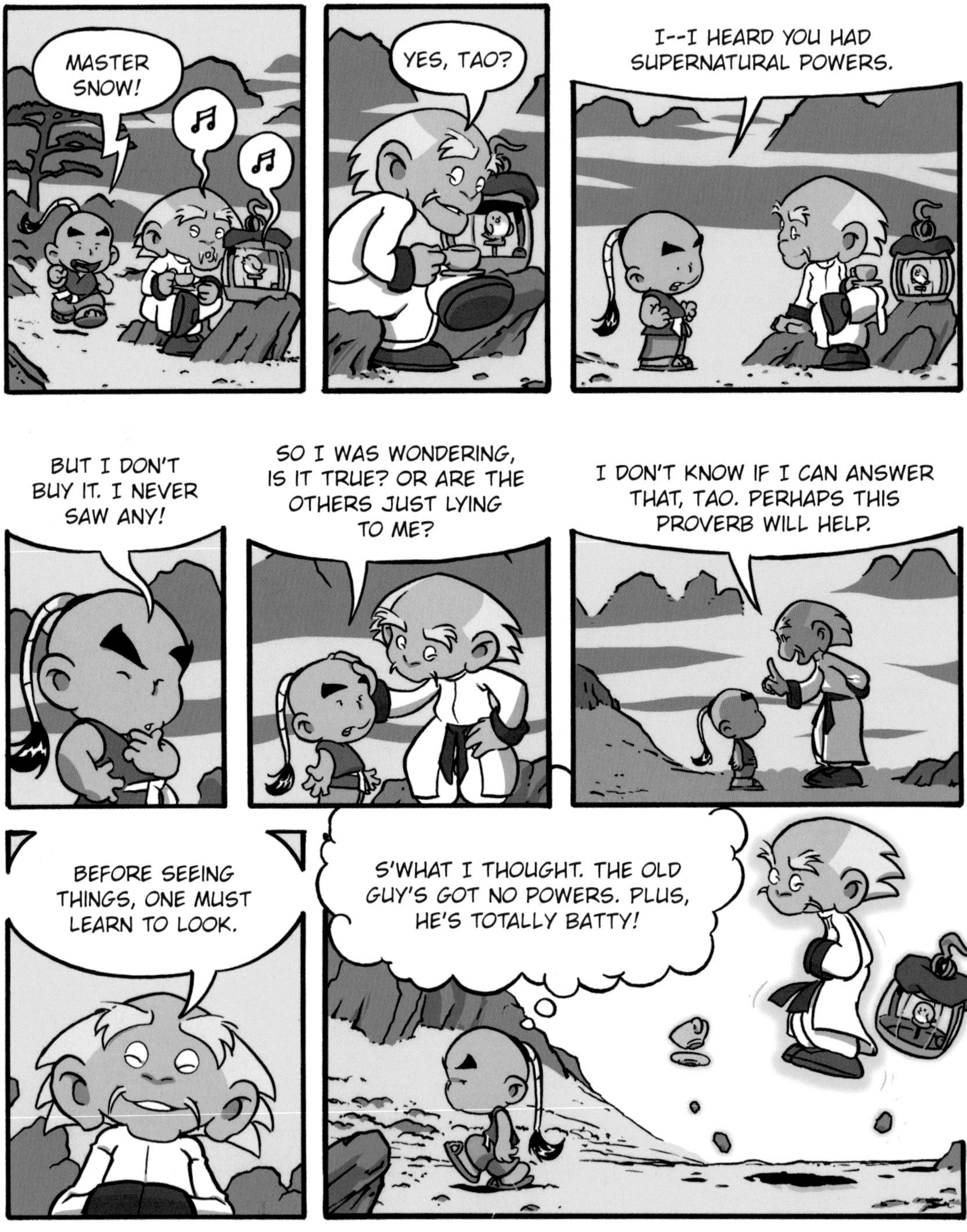

MASTER SNOW!
YES, TAO?
I--I HEARD YOU HAD SUPERNATURAL POWERS.
BUT I DON'T BUY IT. I NEVER SAW ANY!
SO I WAS WONDERING, IS IT TRUE? OR ARE THE OTHERS JUST LYING TO ME?
I DON'T KNOW IF I CAN ANSWER THAT, TAO. PERHAPS THIS PROVERB WILL HELP.
BEFORE SEEING THINGS, ONE MUST LEARN TO LOOK.
S'WHAT I THOUGHT. THE OLD GUY'S GOT NO POWERS. PLUS, HE'S TOTALLY BATTY!

A Samurai Must Know How to Improvise

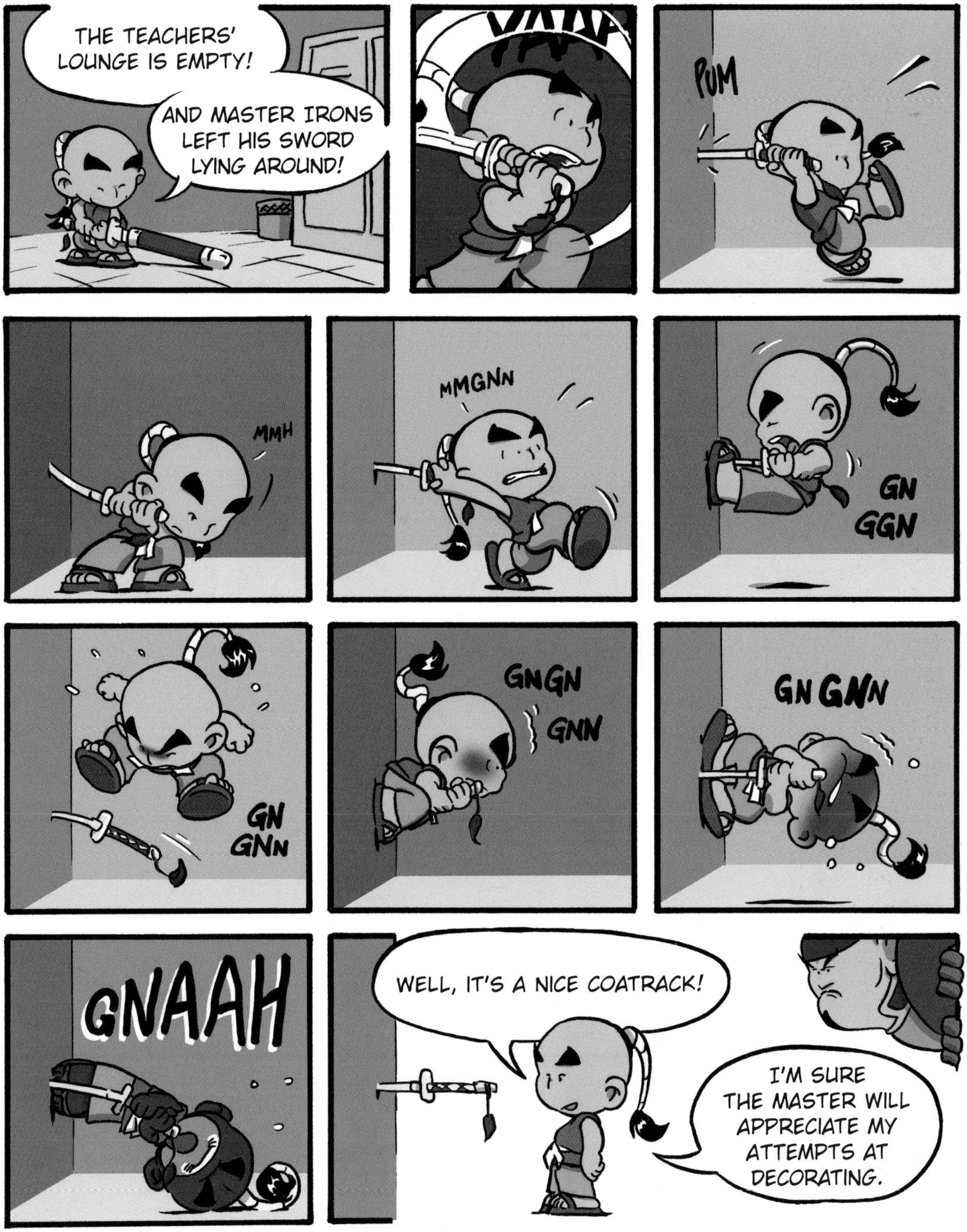
THE TEACHERS' LOUNGE IS EMPTY!
AND MASTER IRONS LEFT HIS SWORD LYING AROUND!
PUM
MMH
MMGNN
GN GGN
GN GNN
GNGN GNN
GN GNN
GNAAH
WELL, IT'S A NICE COATRACK!
I'M SURE THE MASTER WILL APPRECIATE MY ATTEMPTS AT DECORATING.

The Many Uses of a Young Imagination

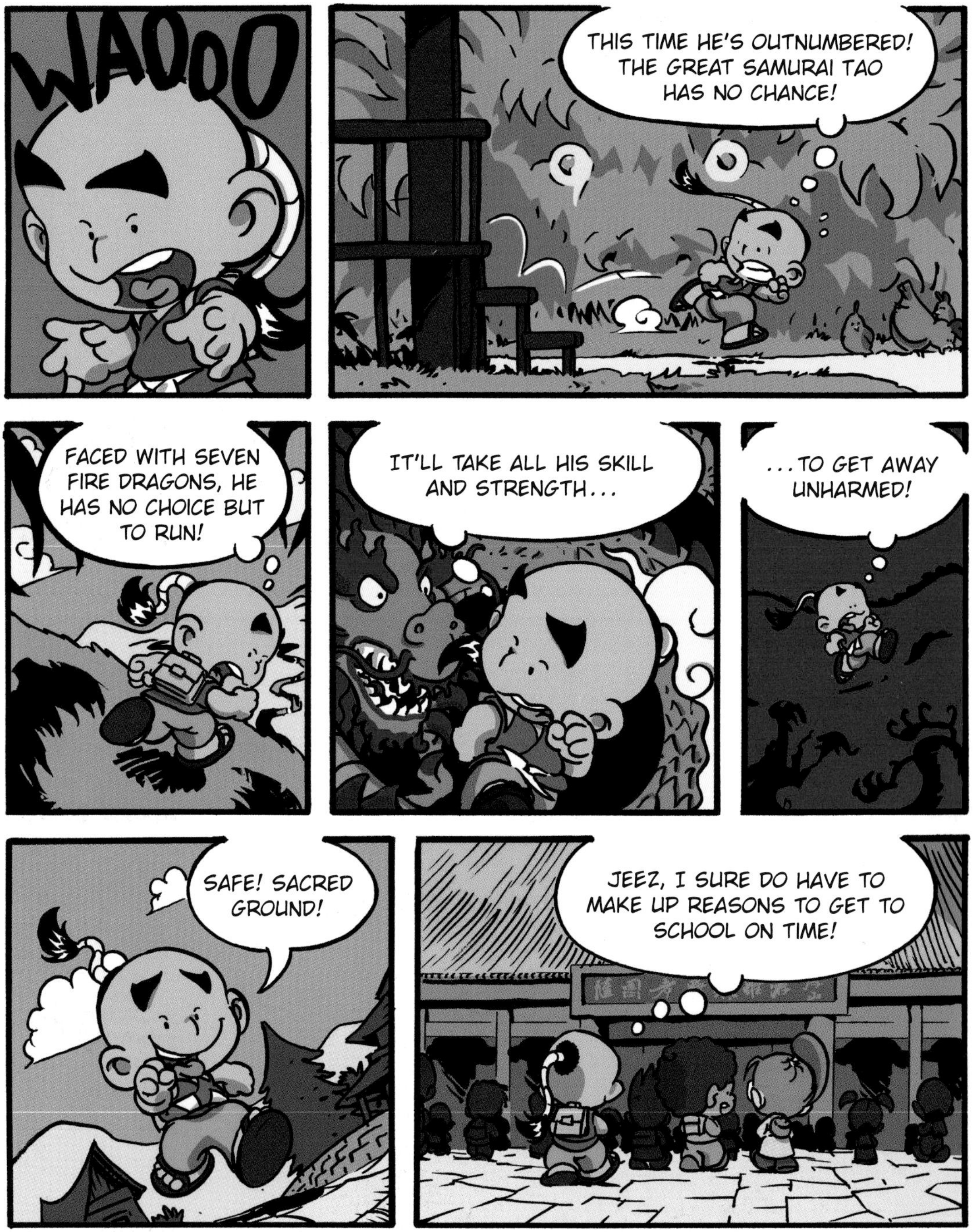

WAOOO
THIS TIME HE'S OUTNUMBERED! THE GREAT SAMURAI TAO HAS NO CHANCE!
FACED WITH SEVEN FIRE DRAGONS, HE HAS NO CHOICE BUT TO RUN!
IT'LL TAKE ALL HIS SKILL AND STRENGTH...
...TO GET AWAY UNHARMED!
SAFE! SACRED GROUND!
JEEZ, I SURE DO HAVE TO MAKE UP REASONS TO GET TO SCHOOL ON TIME!

He Who Cannot Fly Must Avoid Falling

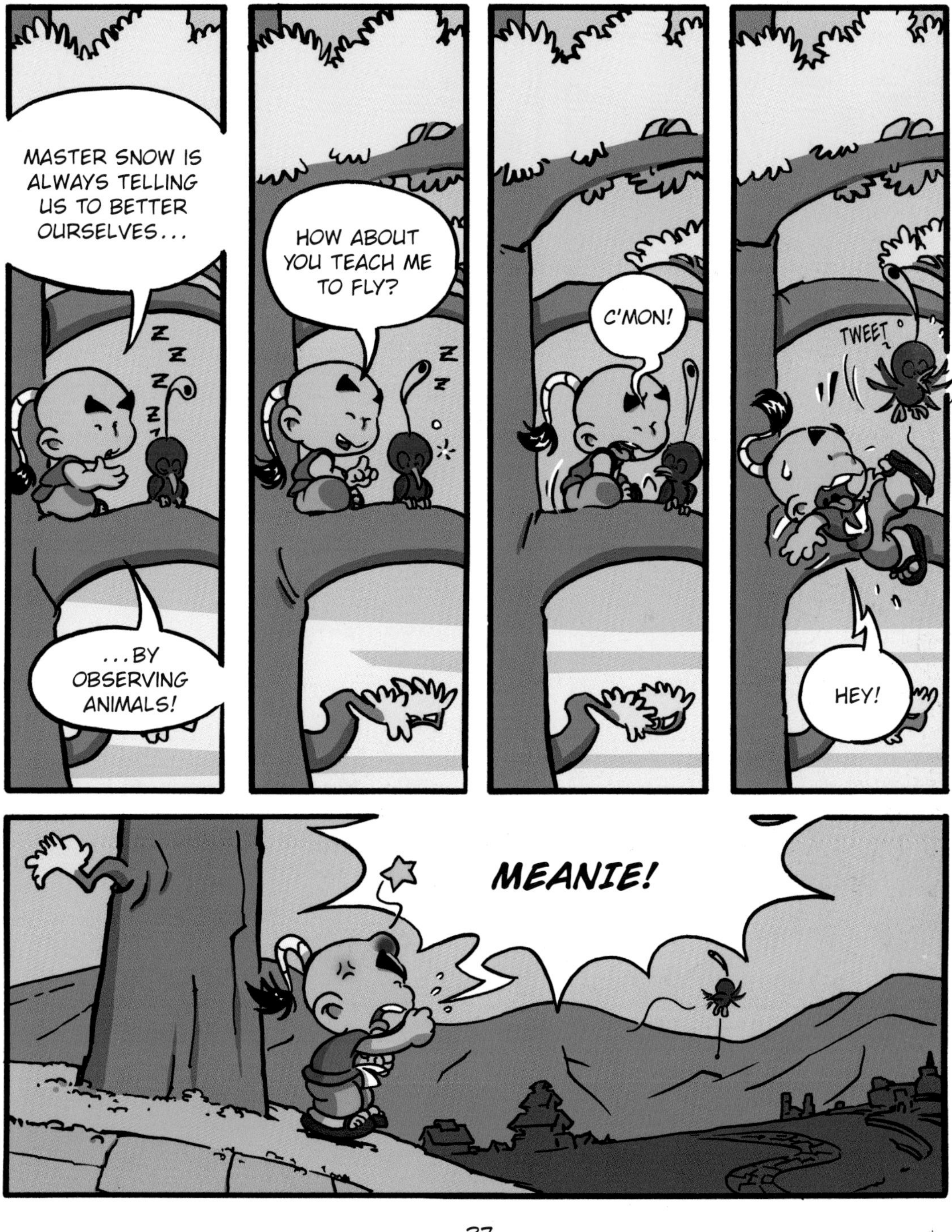

MASTER SNOW IS ALWAYS TELLING US TO BETTER OURSELVES...
...BY OBSERVING ANIMALS!
Z Z Z Z Z
HOW ABOUT YOU TEACH ME TO FLY?
Z Z
C'MON!
TWEET
HEY!
MEANIE!

The Longest Route Is Not Always the Best

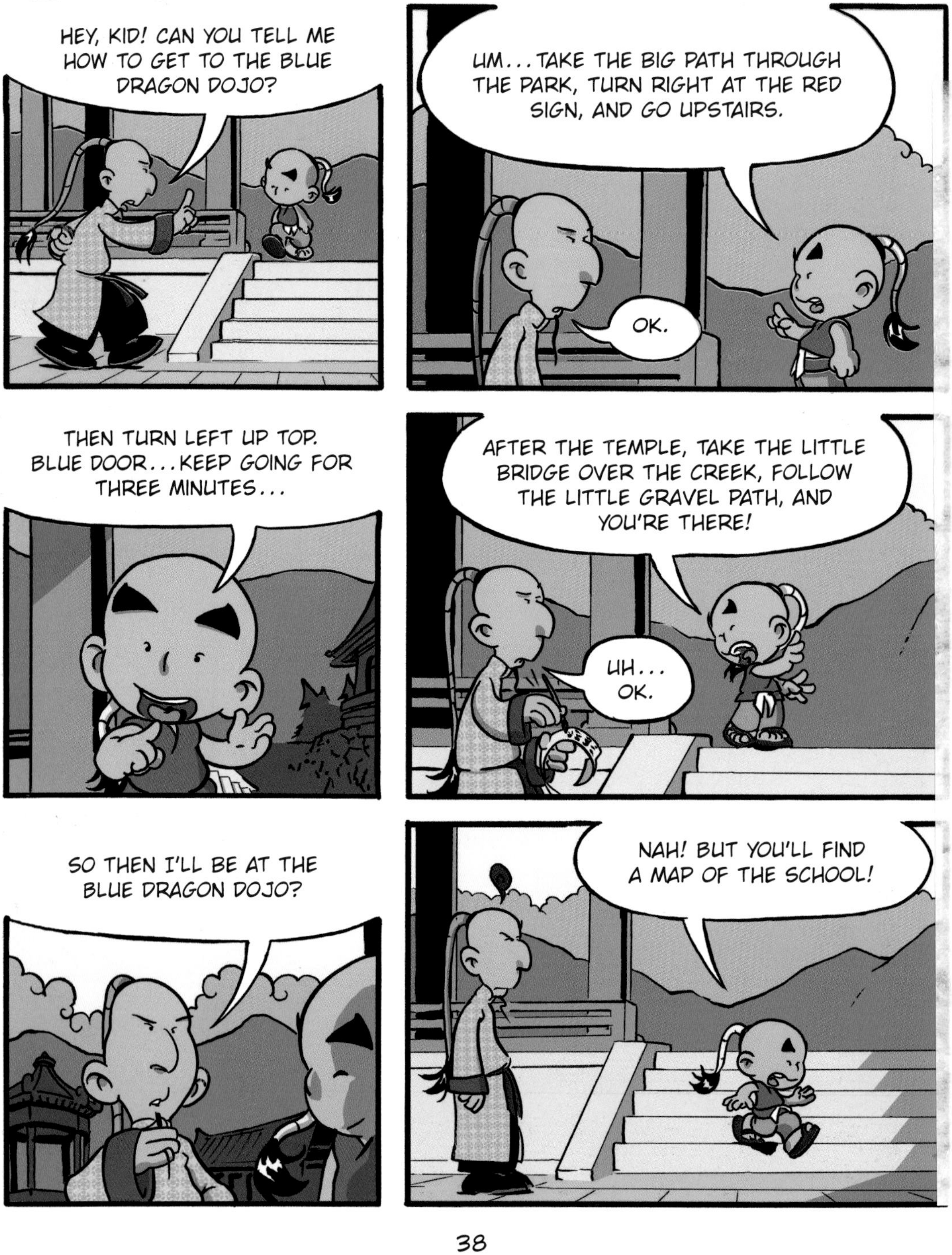
HEY, KID! CAN YOU TELL ME HOW TO GET TO THE BLUE DRAGON DOJO?
UM...TAKE THE BIG PATH THROUGH THE PARK, TURN RIGHT AT THE RED SIGN, AND GO UPSTAIRS.
OK.
THEN TURN LEFT UP TOP. BLUE DOOR...KEEP GOING FOR THREE MINUTES...
AFTER THE TEMPLE, TAKE THE LITTLE BRIDGE OVER THE CREEK, FOLLOW THE LITTLE GRAVEL PATH, AND YOU'RE THERE!
UH... OK.
SO THEN I'LL BE AT THE BLUE DRAGON DOJO?
NAH! BUT YOU'LL FIND A MAP OF THE SCHOOL!

Missing the Point

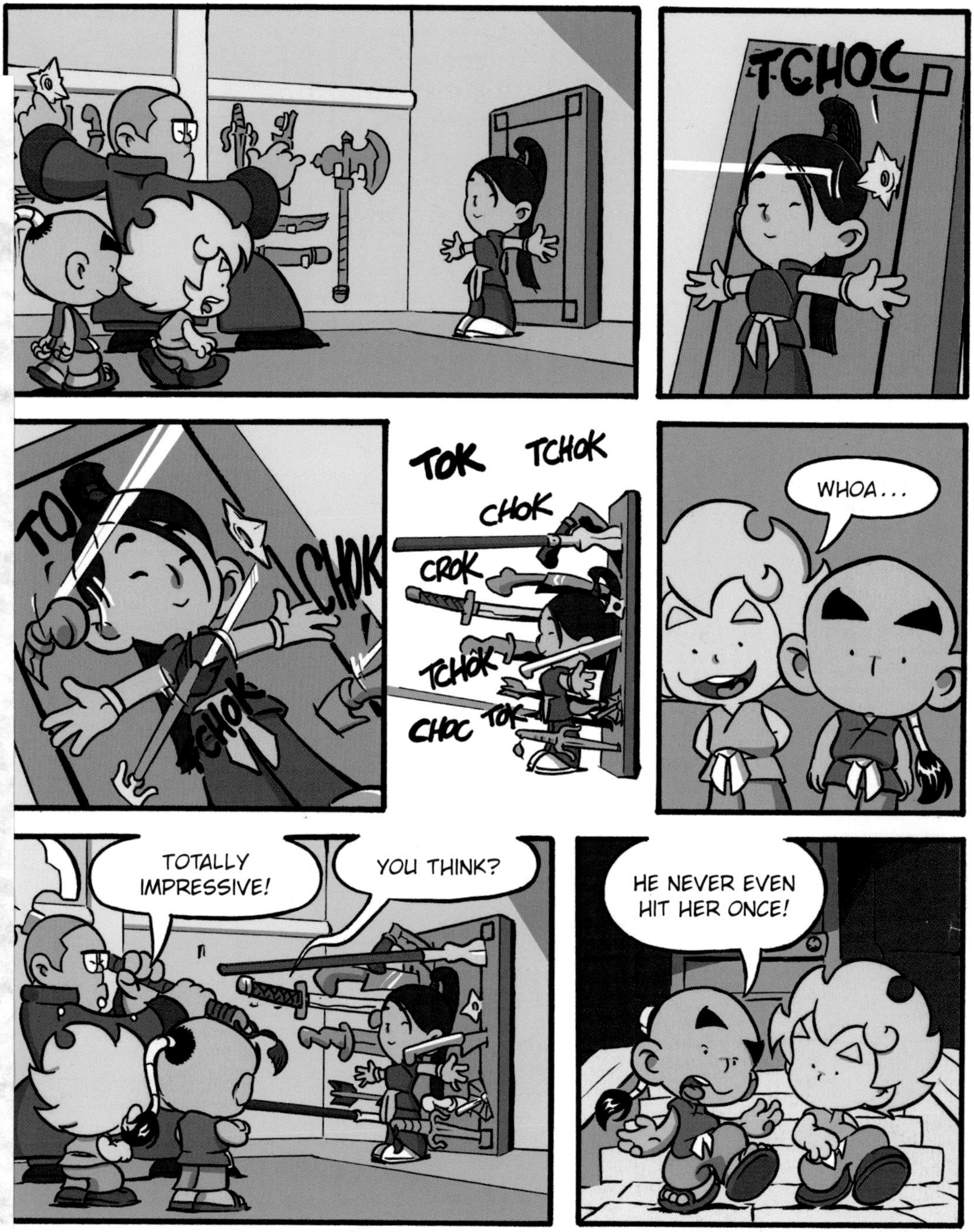
TCHOC
TOK
CHOK
CHOK
TOK
TCHOK
CHOK
CROK
TCHOK
CHOC
TOK
WHOA...
TOTALLY IMPRESSIVE!
YOU THINK?
HE NEVER EVEN HIT HER ONCE!

The Clever Fox Will Always Fool the Simple Pigeon

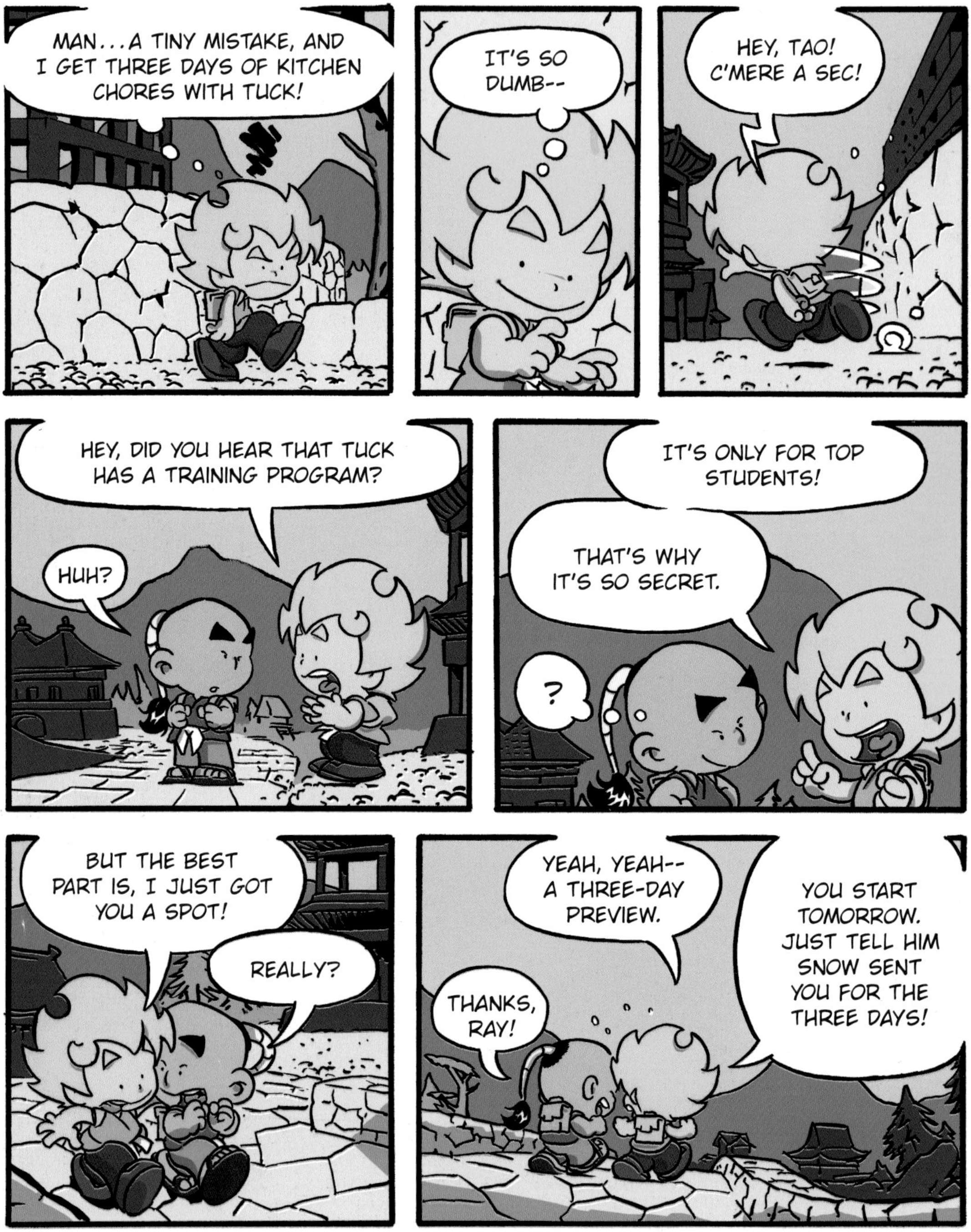
MAN...A TINY MISTAKE, AND I GET THREE DAYS OF KITCHEN CHORES WITH TUCK!
IT'S SO DUMB--
HEY, TAO! C'MERE A SEC!
HEY, DID YOU HEAR THAT TUCK HAS A TRAINING PROGRAM?
HUH?
IT'S ONLY FOR TOP STUDENTS!
THAT'S WHY IT'S SO SECRET.
?
BUT THE BEST PART IS, I JUST GOT YOU A SPOT!
REALLY?
YEAH, YEAH-- A THREE-DAY PREVIEW.
YOU START TOMORROW. JUST TELL HIM SNOW SENT YOU FOR THE THREE DAYS!
THANKS, RAY!

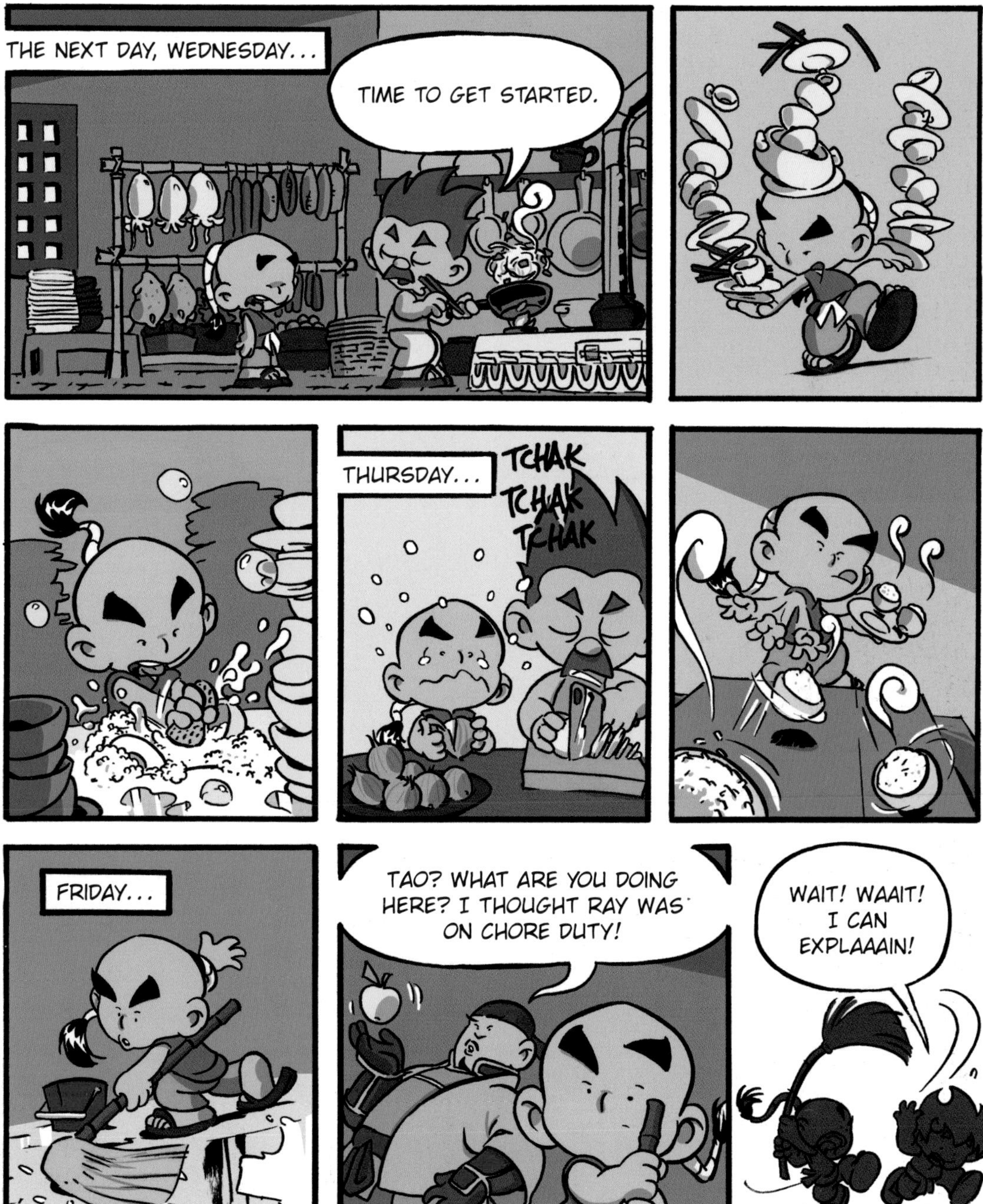
THE NEXT DAY, WEDNESDAY...
TIME TO GET STARTED.
THURSDAY...
TCHAK
TCHAK
TCHAK
FRIDAY...
TAO? WHAT ARE YOU DOING HERE? I THOUGHT RAY WAS ON CHORE DUTY!
WAIT! WAAIT! I CAN EXPLAAAIN!

Silence Speaks to Those Who Listen

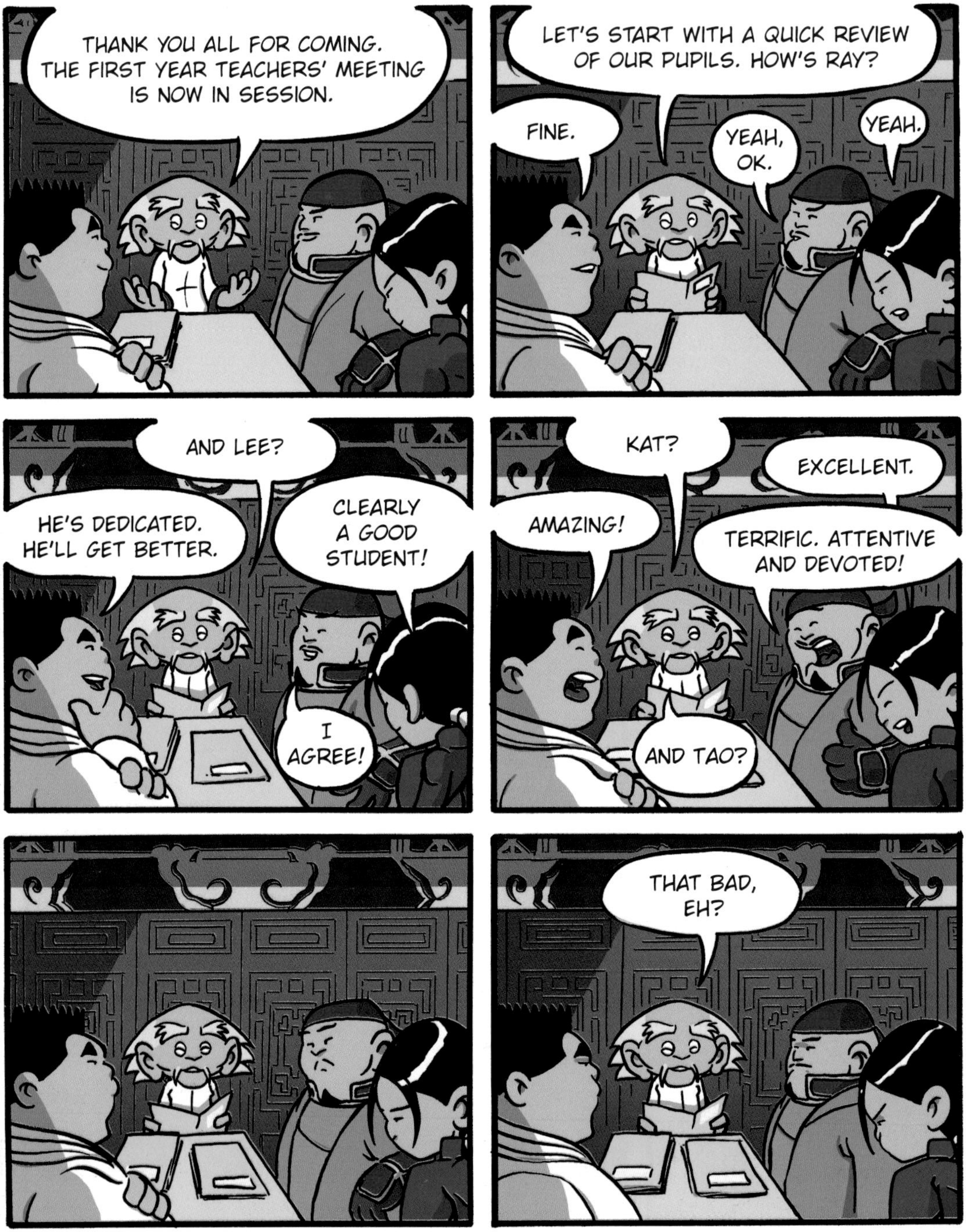
THANK YOU ALL FOR COMING. THE FIRST YEAR TEACHERS' MEETING IS NOW IN SESSION.
LET'S START WITH A QUICK REVIEW OF OUR PUPILS. HOW'S RAY?
FINE.
YEAH, OK.
YEAH.
AND LEE?
HE'S DEDICATED. HE'LL GET BETTER.
CLEARLY A GOOD STUDENT!
I AGREE!
KAT?
EXCELLENT.
AMAZING!
TERRIFIC. ATTENTIVE AND DEVOTED!
AND TAO?
THAT BAD, EH?

Cool as Ice

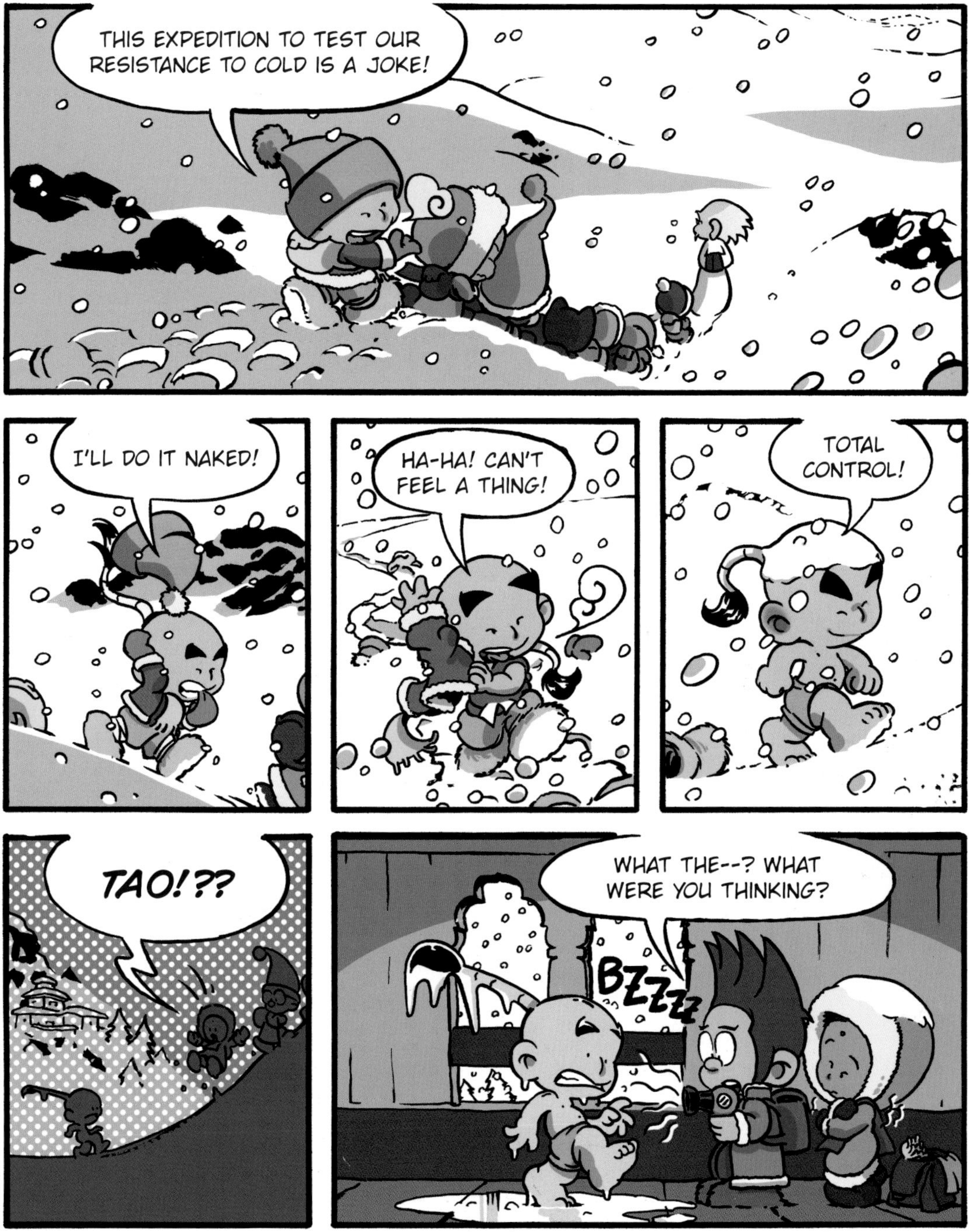
THIS EXPEDITION TO TEST OUR RESISTANCE TO COLD IS A JOKE!
I'LL DO IT NAKED!
HA-HA! CAN'T FEEL A THING!
TOTAL CONTROL!
TAO!??
WHAT THE--? WHAT WERE YOU THINKING?
BZZZZ

A Studious Grasshopper Is Never Late

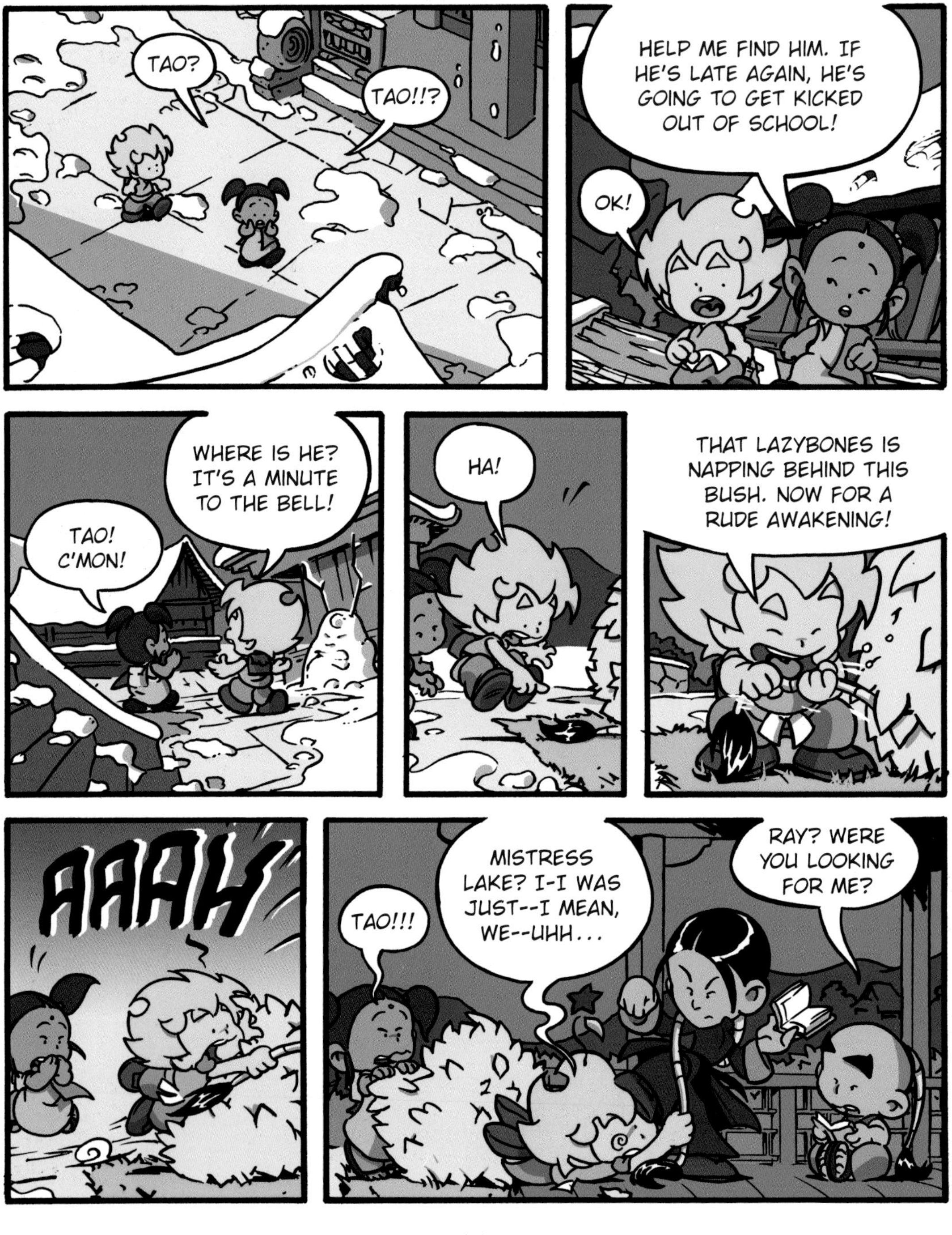
TAO?
TAO!!?
HELP ME FIND HIM. IF HE'S LATE AGAIN, HE'S GOING TO GET KICKED OUT OF SCHOOL!
OK!
WHERE IS HE? IT'S A MINUTE TO THE BELL!
TAO! C'MON!
HA!
THAT LAZYBONES IS NAPPING BEHIND THIS BUSH. NOW FOR A RUDE AWAKENING!
AAAH
TAO!!!
MISTRESS LAKE? I-I WAS JUST--I MEAN, WE--UHH...
RAY? WERE YOU LOOKING FOR ME?

The Shortest Route Is Not Always the Best

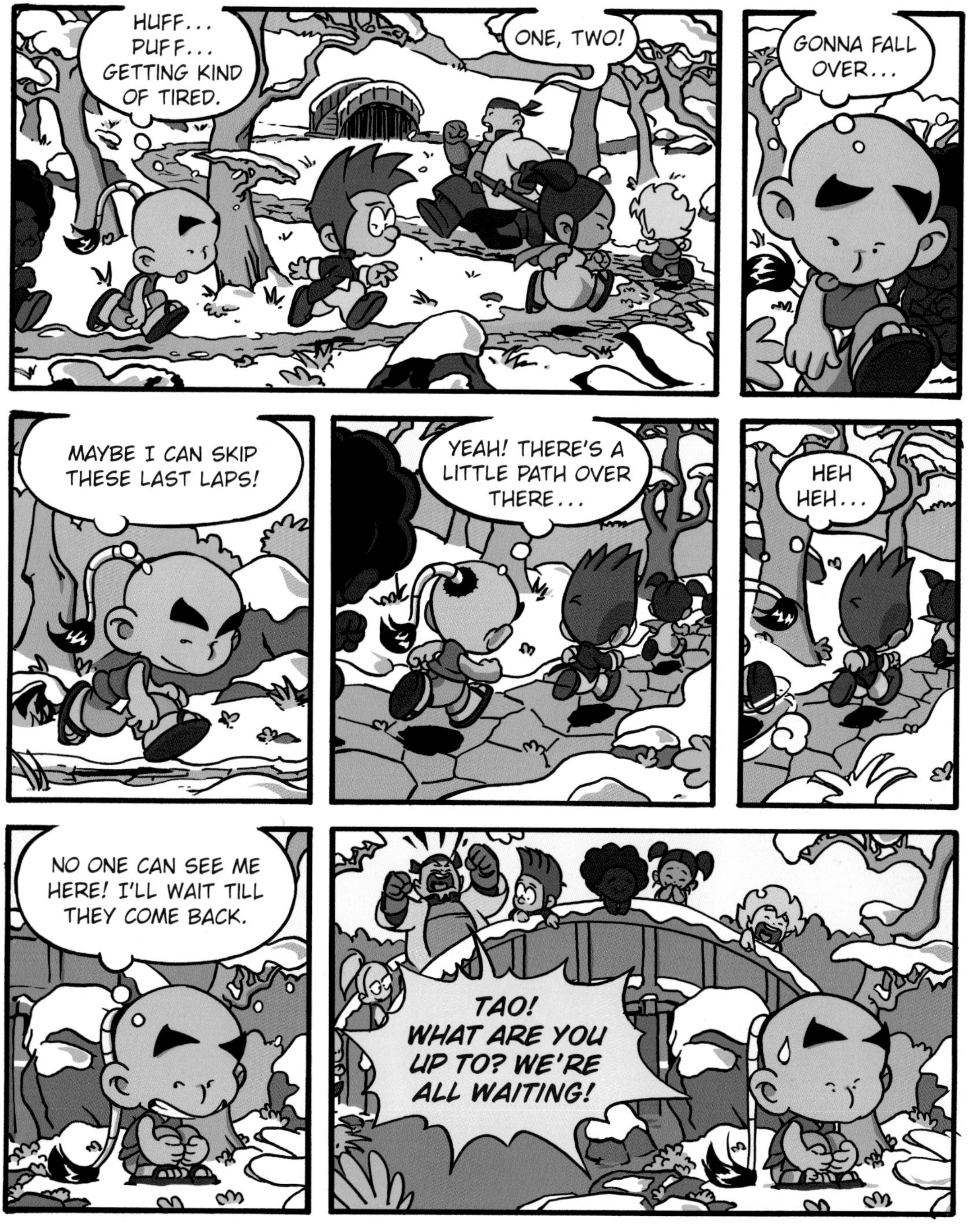
HUFF... PUFF... GETTING KIND OF TIRED.
ONE, TWO!
GONNA FALL OVER...
MAYBE I CAN SKIP THESE LAST LAPS!
YEAH! THERE'S A LITTLE PATH OVER THERE...
HEH HEH...
NO ONE CAN SEE ME HERE! I'LL WAIT TILL THEY COME BACK.
TAO! WHAT ARE YOU UP TO? WE'RE ALL WAITING!

A True Fighter Knows No Rest

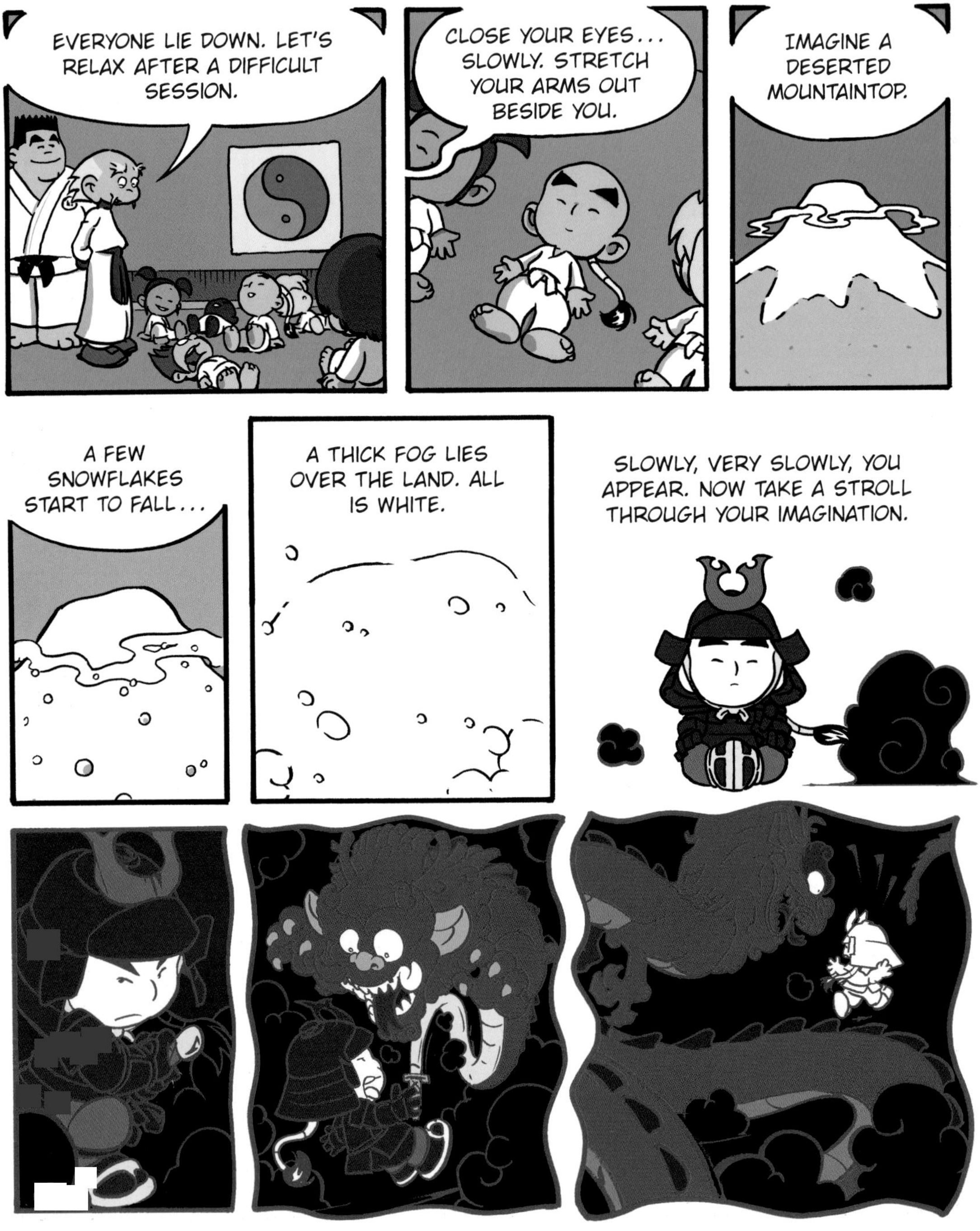
EVERYONE LIE DOWN. LET'S RELAX AFTER A DIFFICULT SESSION.
CLOSE YOUR EYES . . . SLOWLY. STRETCH YOUR ARMS OUT BESIDE YOU.
IMAGINE A DESERTED MOUNTAINTOP.
A FEW SNOWFLAKES START TO FALL . . .
A THICK FOG LIES OVER THE LAND. ALL IS WHITE.
SLOWLY, VERY SLOWLY, YOU APPEAR. NOW TAKE A STROLL THROUGH YOUR IMAGINATION.

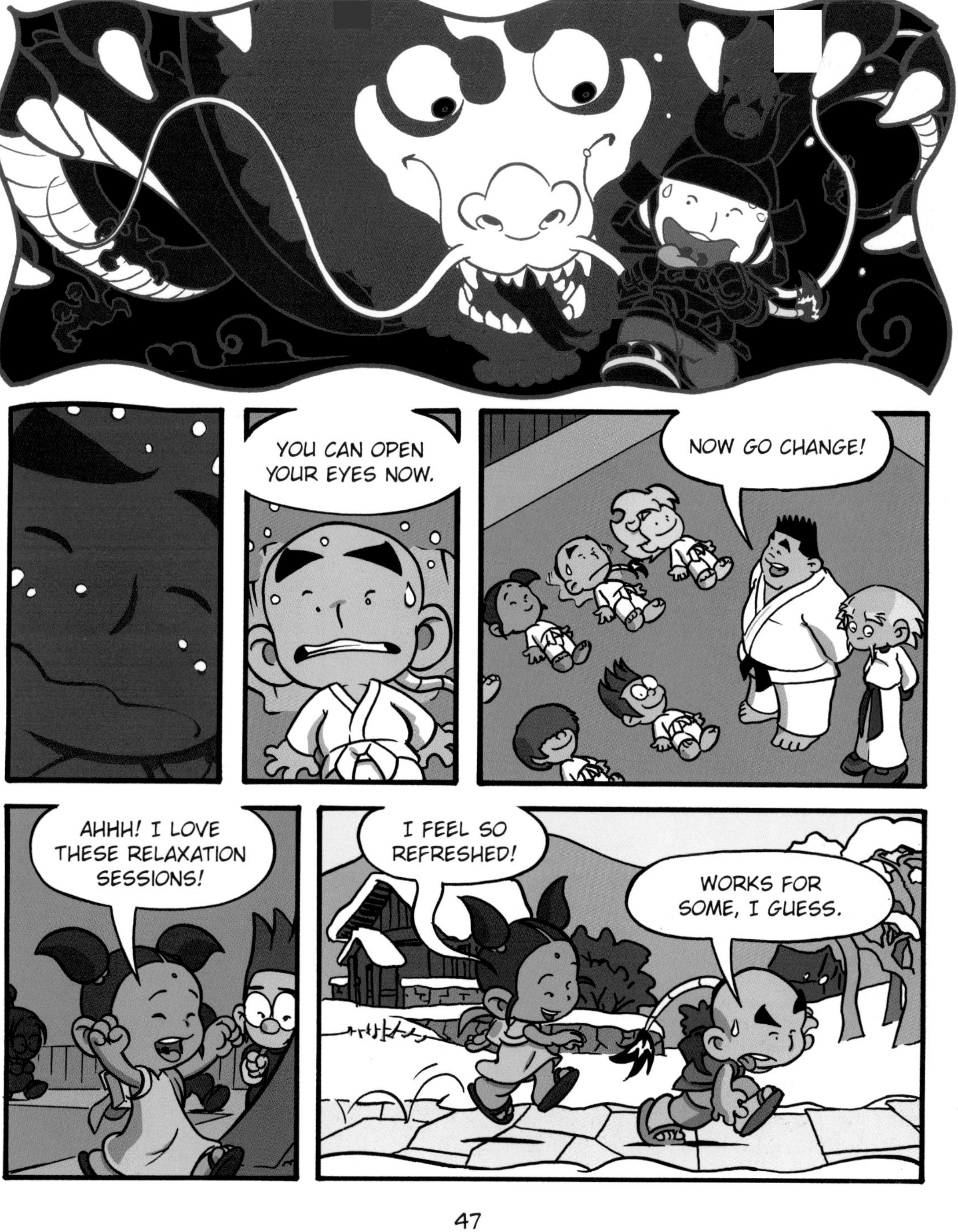
YOU CAN OPEN YOUR EYES NOW.
NOW GO CHANGE!
AHHH! I LOVE THESE RELAXATION SESSIONS!
I FEEL SO REFRESHED!
WORKS FOR SOME, I GUESS.

The Bullheaded Must Be Thick-Skulled

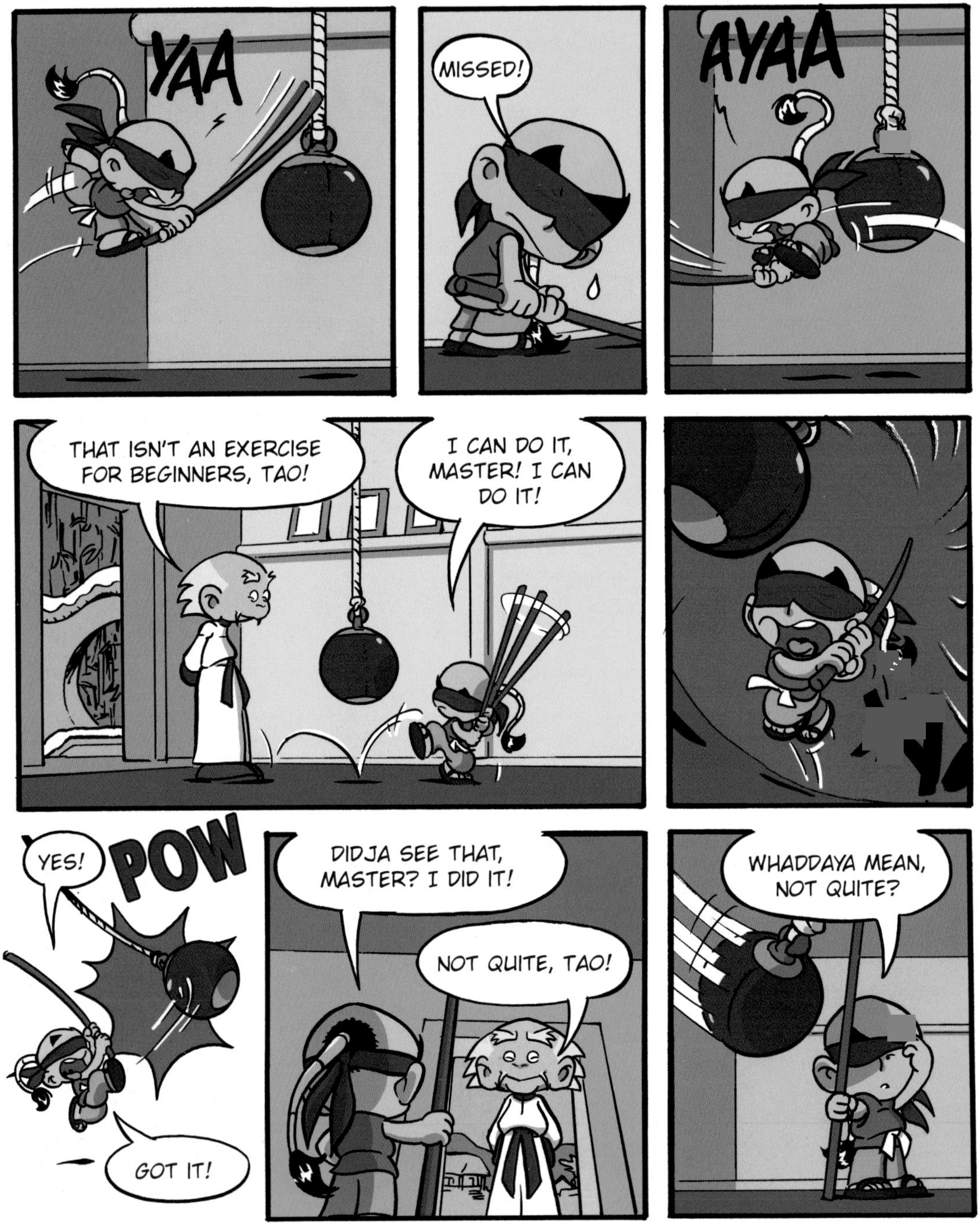
YAA
MISSED!
AYAA
THAT ISN'T AN EXERCISE FOR BEGINNERS, TAO!
I CAN DO IT, MASTER! I CAN DO IT!
YES!
POW
GOT IT!
DIDJA SEE THAT, MASTER? I DID IT!
NOT QUITE, TAO!
WHADDAYA MEAN, NOT QUITE?

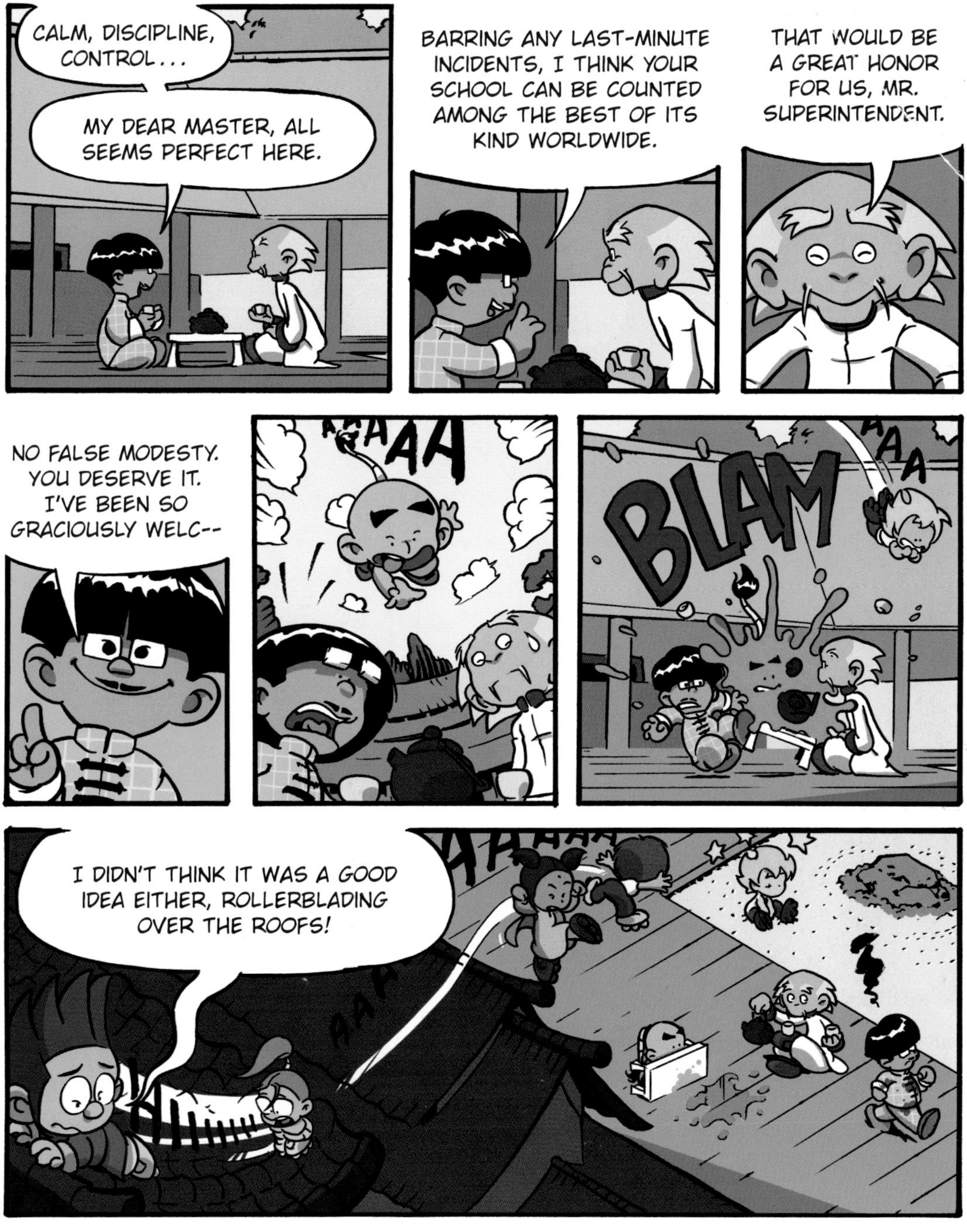
CALM, DISCIPLINE, CONTROL...
MY DEAR MASTER, ALL SEEMS PERFECT HERE.
BARRING ANY LAST-MINUTE INCIDENTS, I THINK YOUR SCHOOL CAN BE COUNTED AMONG THE BEST OF ITS KIND WORLDWIDE.
THAT WOULD BE A GREAT HONOR FOR US, MR. SUPERINTENDENT.
NO FALSE MODESTY. YOU DESERVE IT. I'VE BEEN SO GRACIOUSLY WELC--
AAAA
BLAM
AAA
I DIDN'T THINK IT WAS A GOOD IDEA EITHER, ROLLERBLADING OVER THE ROOFS!
AAAAA

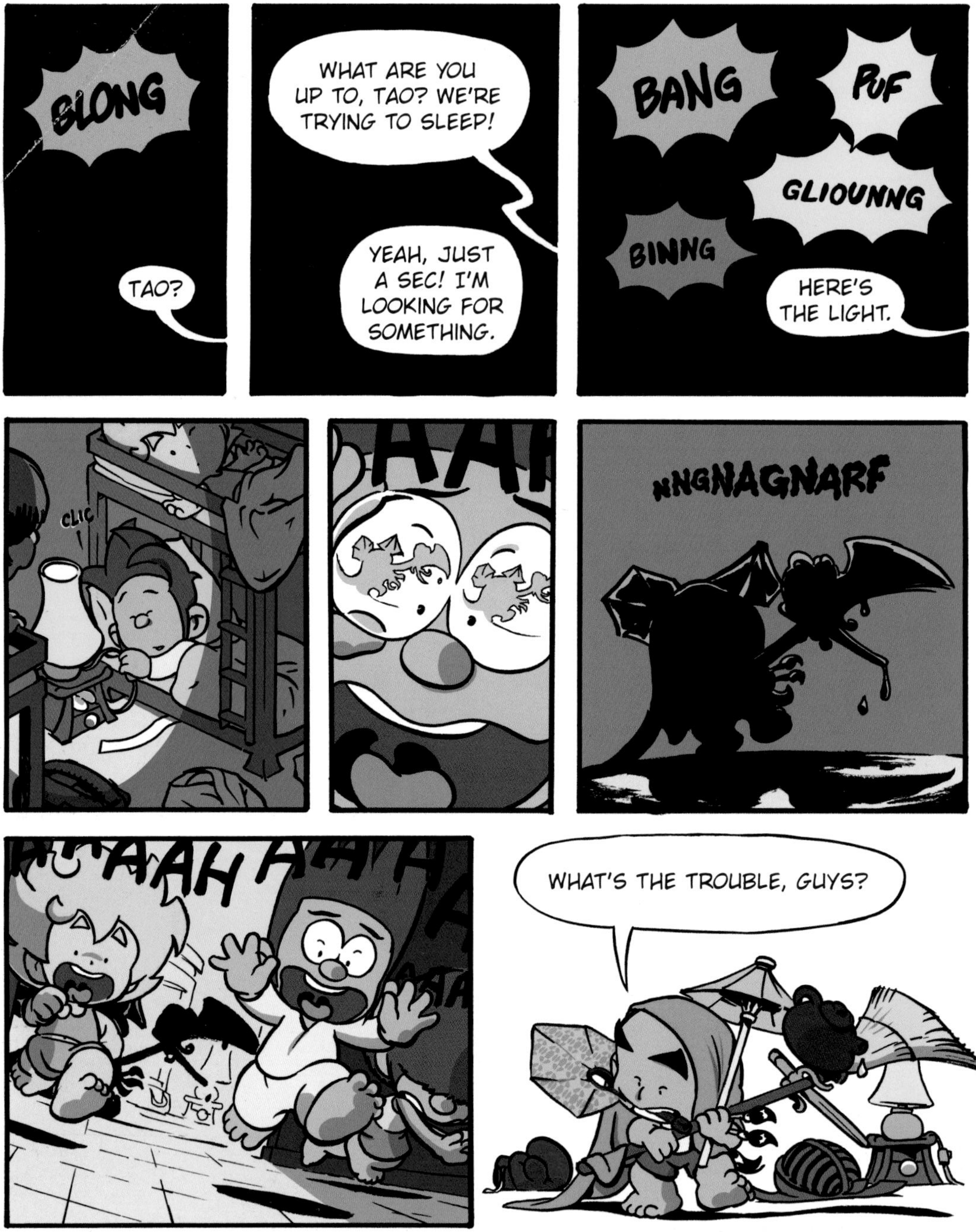
BLONG
TAO?
WHAT ARE YOU UP TO, TAO? WE'RE TRYING TO SLEEP!
YEAH, JUST A SEC! I'M LOOKING FOR SOMETHING.
BANG
PUF
GLIOUNNG
BINNG
HERE'S THE LIGHT.
CLIC
NNGNAGNARF
WHAT'S THE TROUBLE, GUYS?

The Fastest Fish Wins the Race

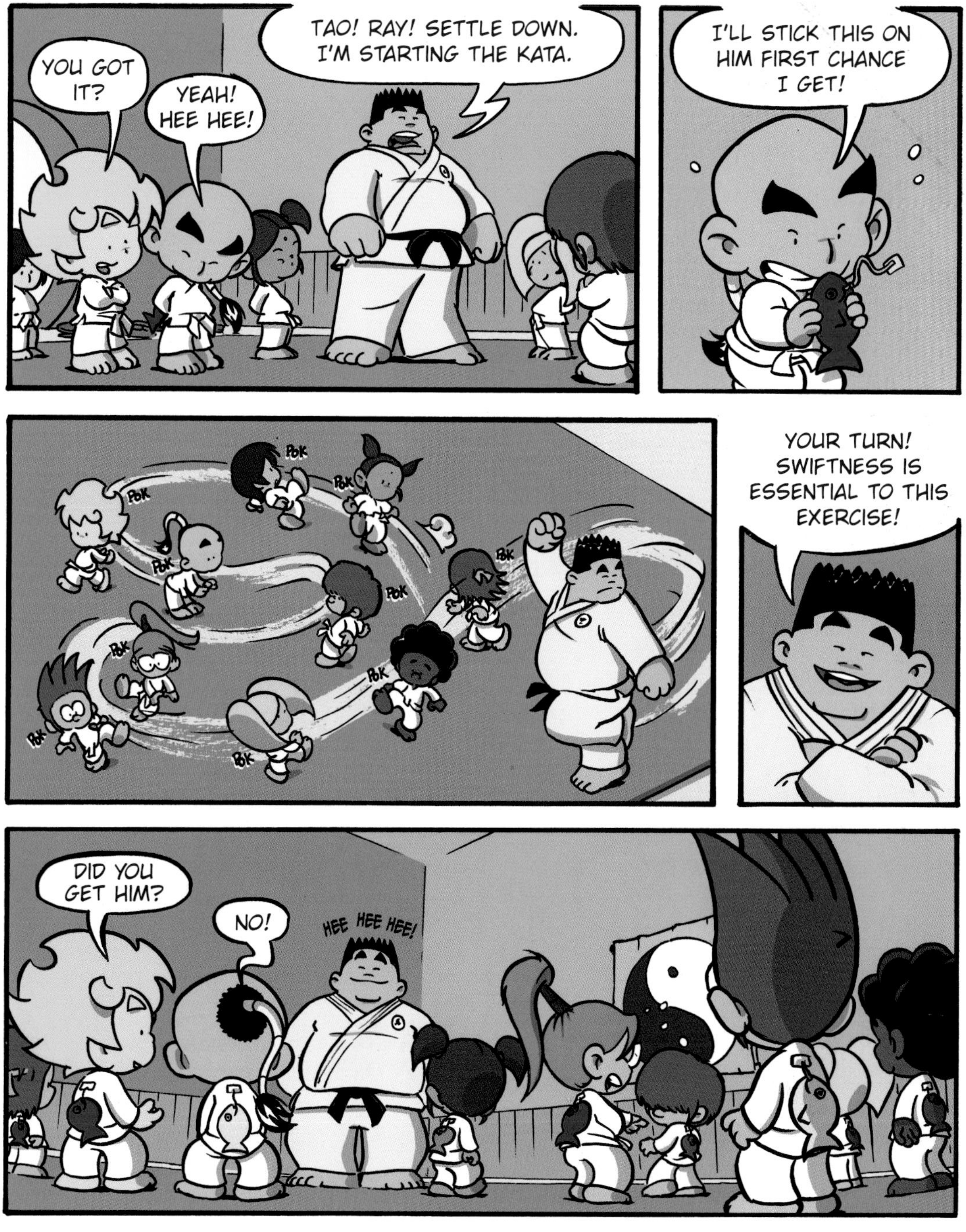
YOU GOT IT?
YEAH! HEE HEE!
TAO! RAY! SETTLE DOWN. I'M STARTING THE KATA.
I'LL STICK THIS ON HIM FIRST CHANCE I GET!
POK
POK
POK
POK
POK
POK
POK
POK
POK
POK
YOUR TURN! SWIFTNESS IS ESSENTIAL TO THIS EXERCISE!
DID YOU GET HIM?
NO!
HEE HEE HEE!

Grasshoppers at Play

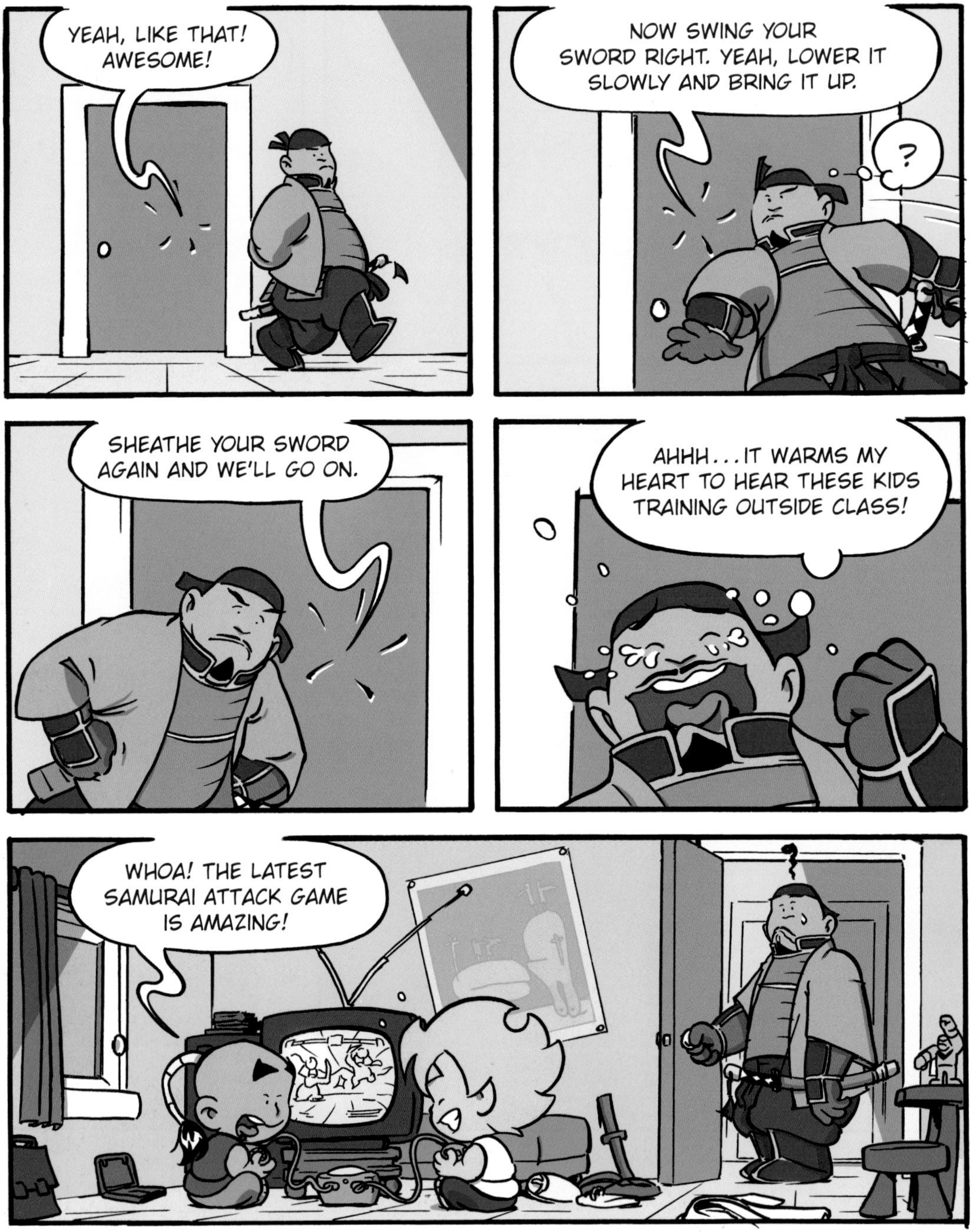
YEAH, LIKE THAT! AWESOME!
NOW SWING YOUR SWORD RIGHT. YEAH, LOWER IT SLOWLY AND BRING IT UP.
?
SHEATHE YOUR SWORD AGAIN AND WE'LL GO ON.
AHHH...IT WARMS MY HEART TO HEAR THESE KIDS TRAINING OUTSIDE CLASS!
WHOA! THE LATEST SAMURAI ATTACK GAME IS AMAZING!

The Impatient Fisherman May Get a Dunking

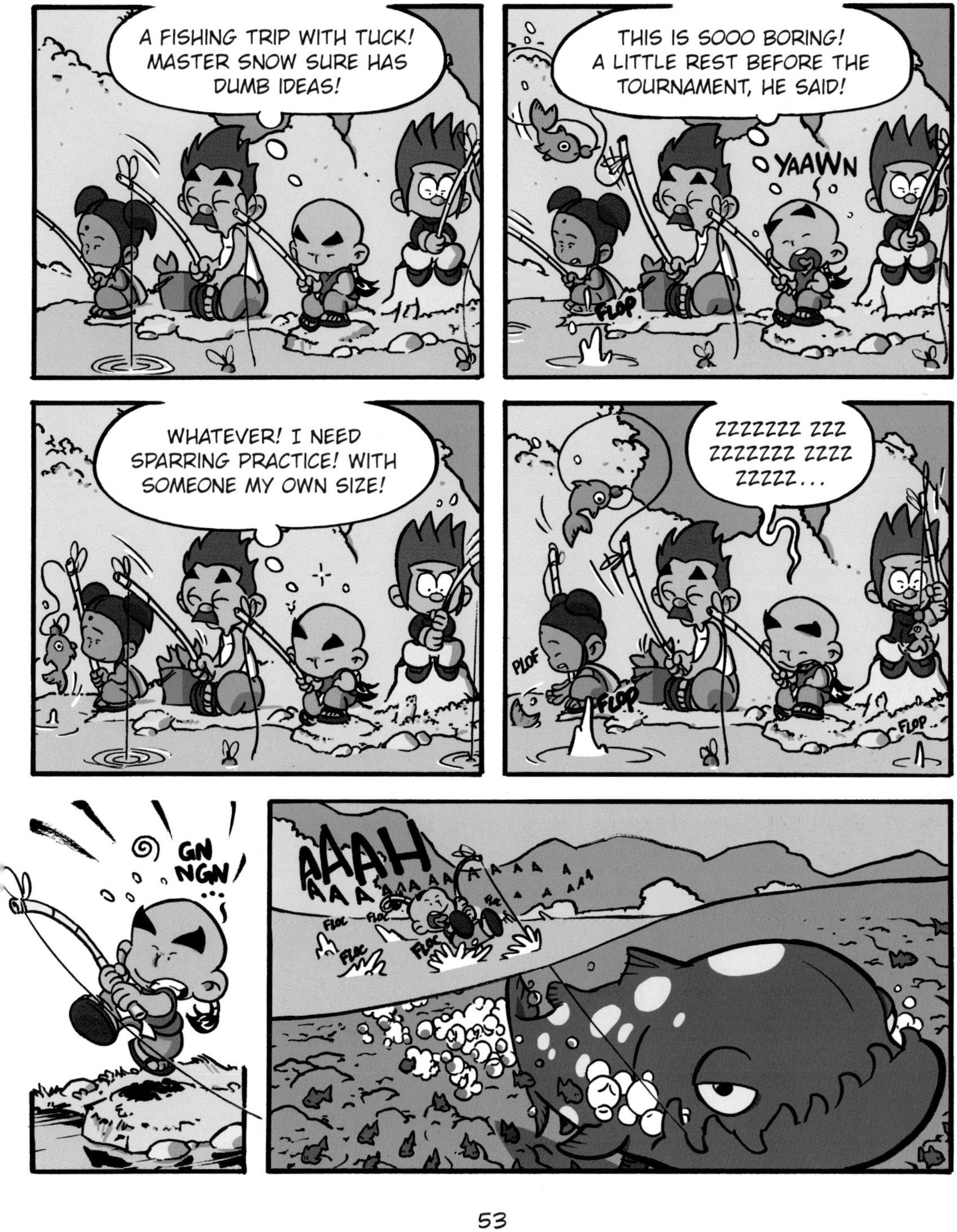

A FISHING TRIP WITH TUCK! MASTER SNOW SURE HAS DUMB IDEAS!
THIS IS SOOO BORING! A LITTLE REST BEFORE THE TOURNAMENT, HE SAID!
YAAWN
FLOP
WHATEVER! I NEED SPARRING PRACTICE! WITH SOMEONE MY OWN SIZE!
ZZZZZZZ ZZZ ZZZZZZZ ZZZZ ZZZZZ...
PLOF
FLOP
FLOP
GN NGN
AAAH
FLOC
FLOC
FLOC
FLOC

It's Raining Swords and Arrows

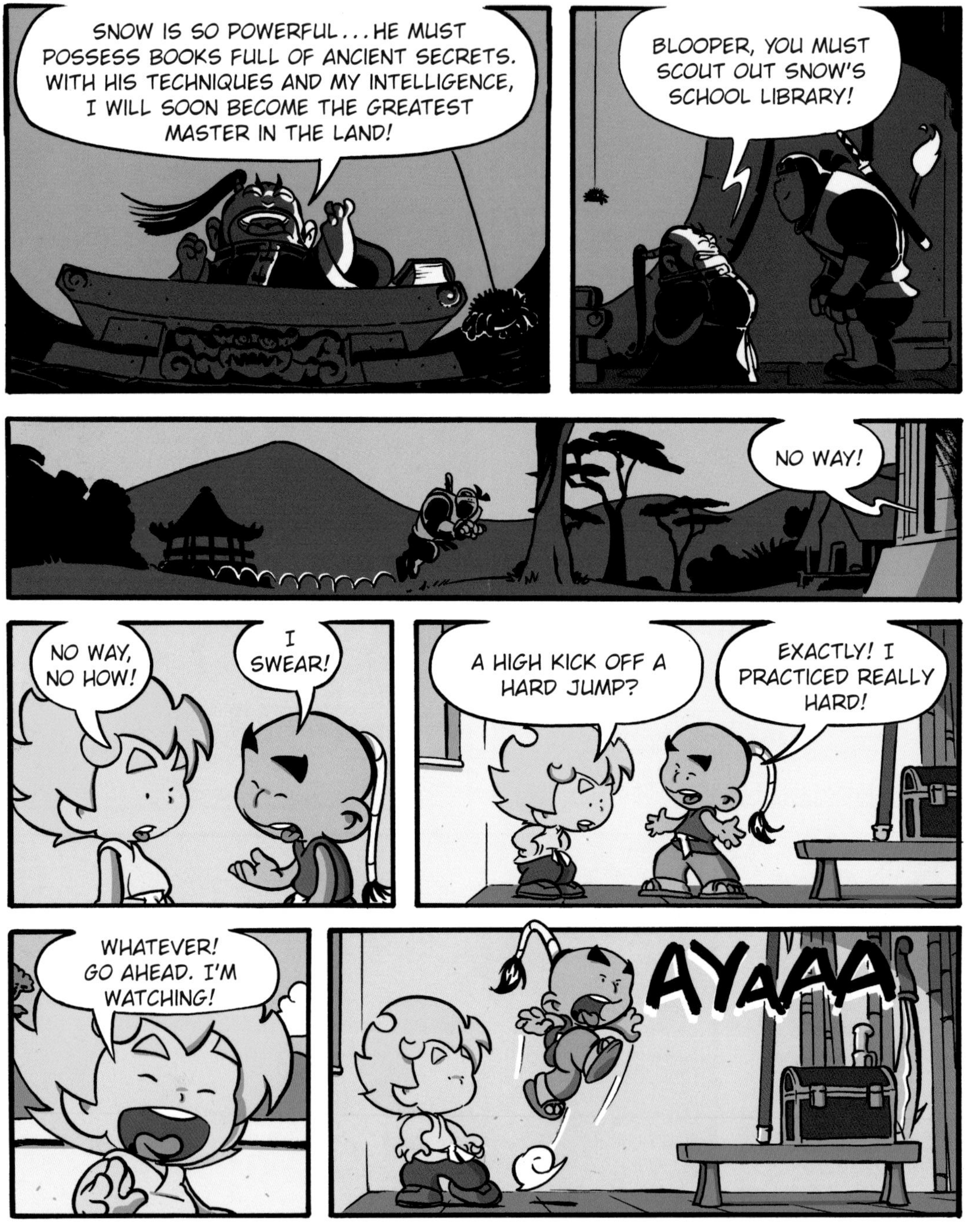
SNOW IS SO POWERFUL . . . HE MUST POSSESS BOOKS FULL OF ANCIENT SECRETS. WITH HIS TECHNIQUES AND MY INTELLIGENCE, I WILL SOON BECOME THE GREATEST MASTER IN THE LAND!
BLOOPER, YOU MUST SCOUT OUT SNOW'S SCHOOL LIBRARY!
NO WAY!
NO WAY, NO HOW!
I SWEAR!
A HIGH KICK OFF A HARD JUMP?
EXACTLY! I PRACTICED REALLY HARD!
WHATEVER! GO AHEAD. I'M WATCHING!
AYAAAA

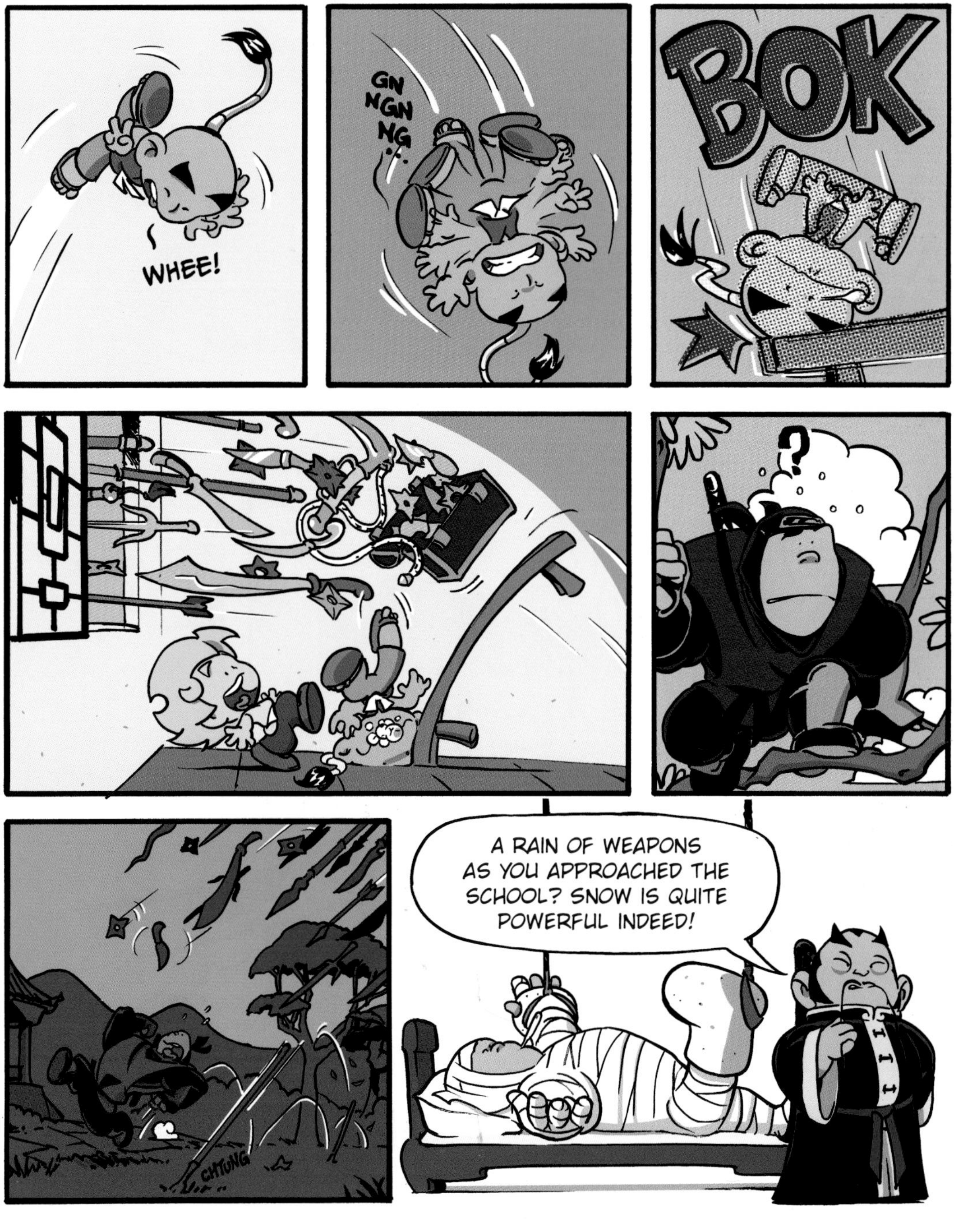
WHEE!
GN NGN NG
BOK
A RAIN OF WEAPONS AS YOU APPROACHED THE SCHOOL? SNOW IS QUITE POWERFUL INDEED!
CHTUNG

A Well-Hidden Little Grasshopper

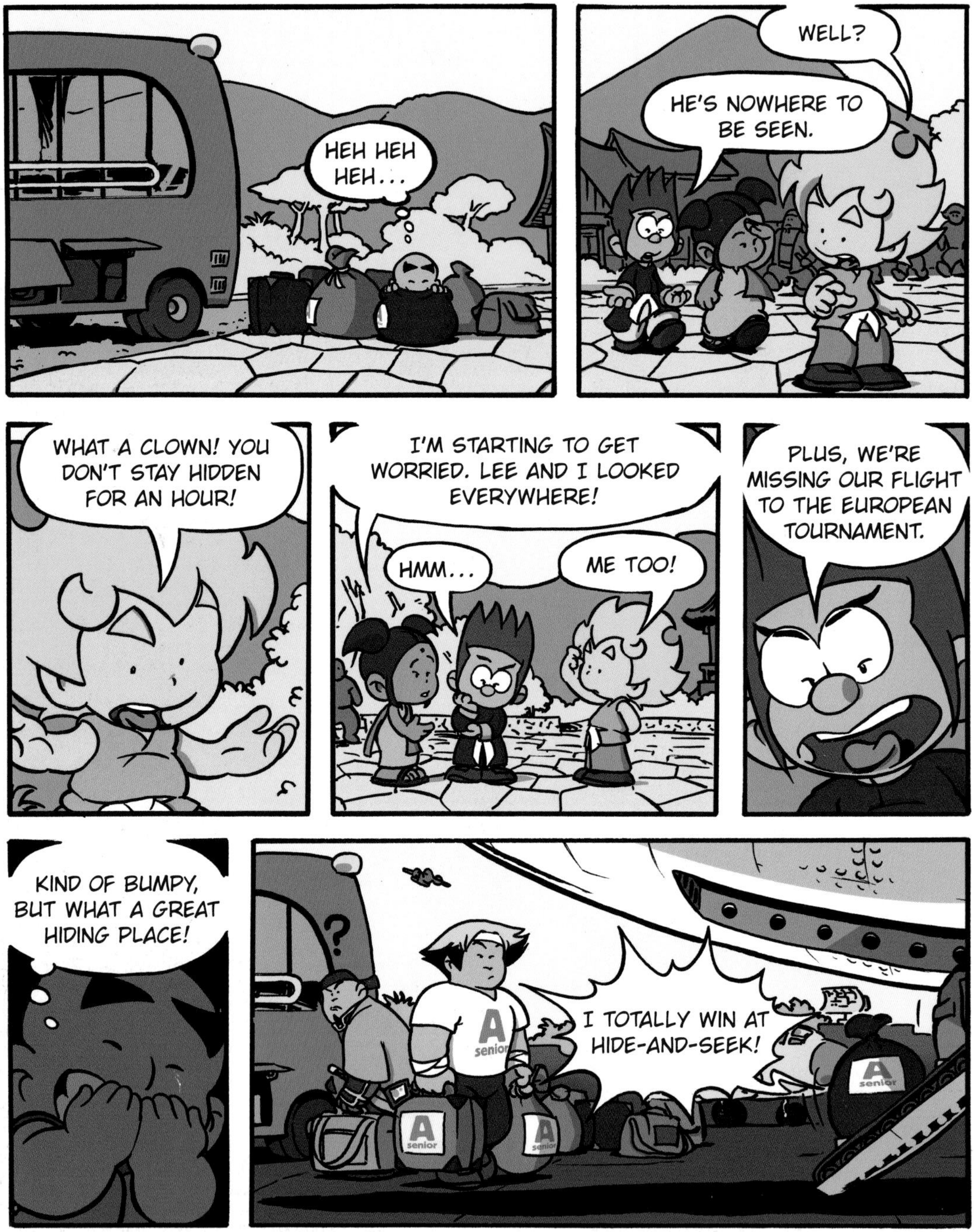
HEH HEH HEH...
WELL?
HE'S NOWHERE TO BE SEEN.
WHAT A CLOWN! YOU DON'T STAY HIDDEN FOR AN HOUR!
I'M STARTING TO GET WORRIED. LEE AND I LOOKED EVERYWHERE!
HMM...
ME TOO!
PLUS, WE'RE MISSING OUR FLIGHT TO THE EUROPEAN TOURNAMENT.
KIND OF BUMPY, BUT WHAT A GREAT HIDING PLACE!
?
I TOTALLY WIN AT HIDE-AND-SEEK!

The Creators of Tao: On the Making of Tao

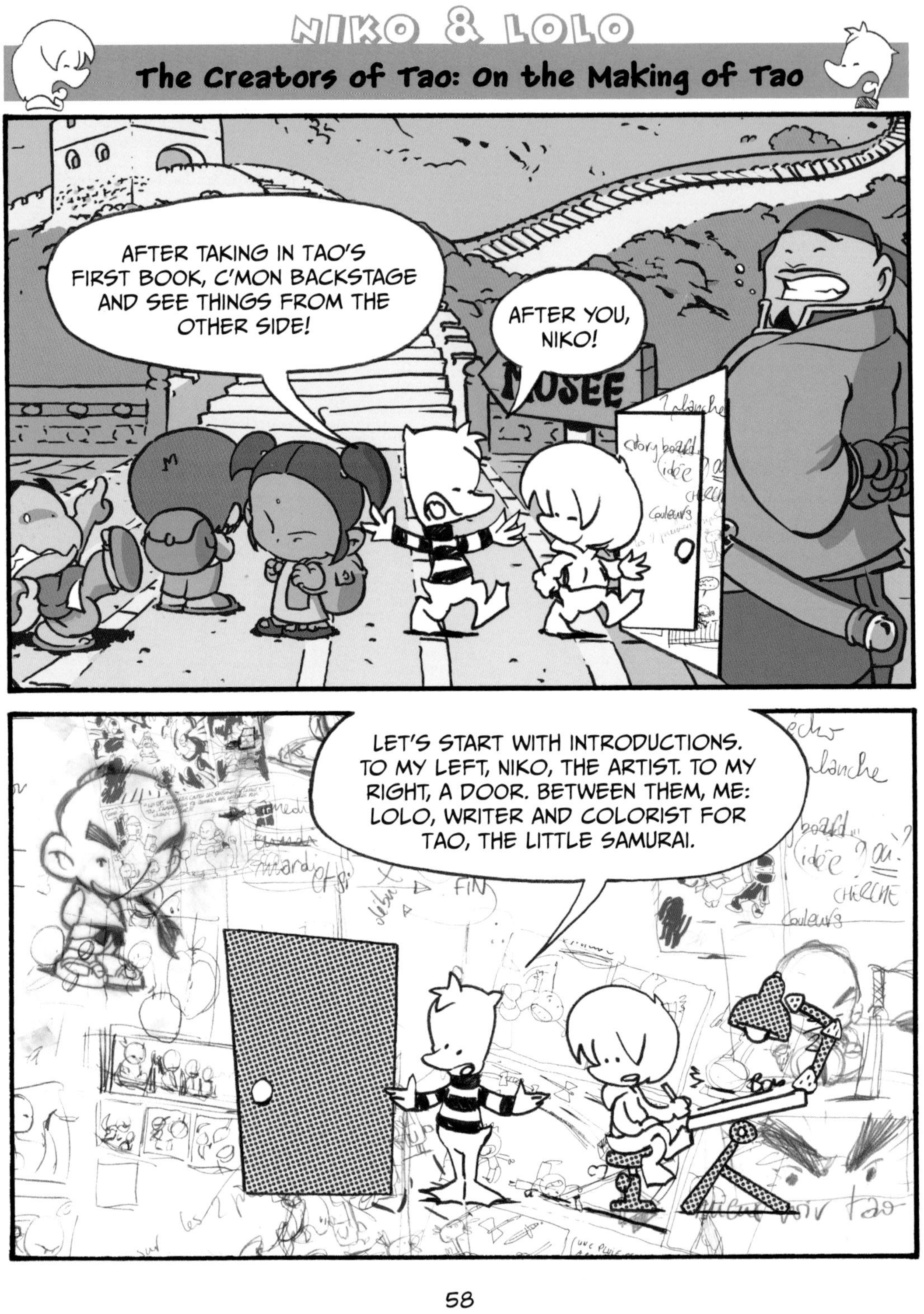
AFTER TAKING IN TAO'S FIRST BOOK, C'MON BACKSTAGE AND SEE THINGS FROM THE OTHER SIDE!
AFTER YOU, NIKO!
LET'S START WITH INTRODUCTIONS. TO MY LEFT, NIKO, THE ARTIST. TO MY RIGHT, A DOOR. BETWEEN THEM, ME: LOLO, WRITER AND COLORIST FOR TAO, THE LITTLE SAMURAI.

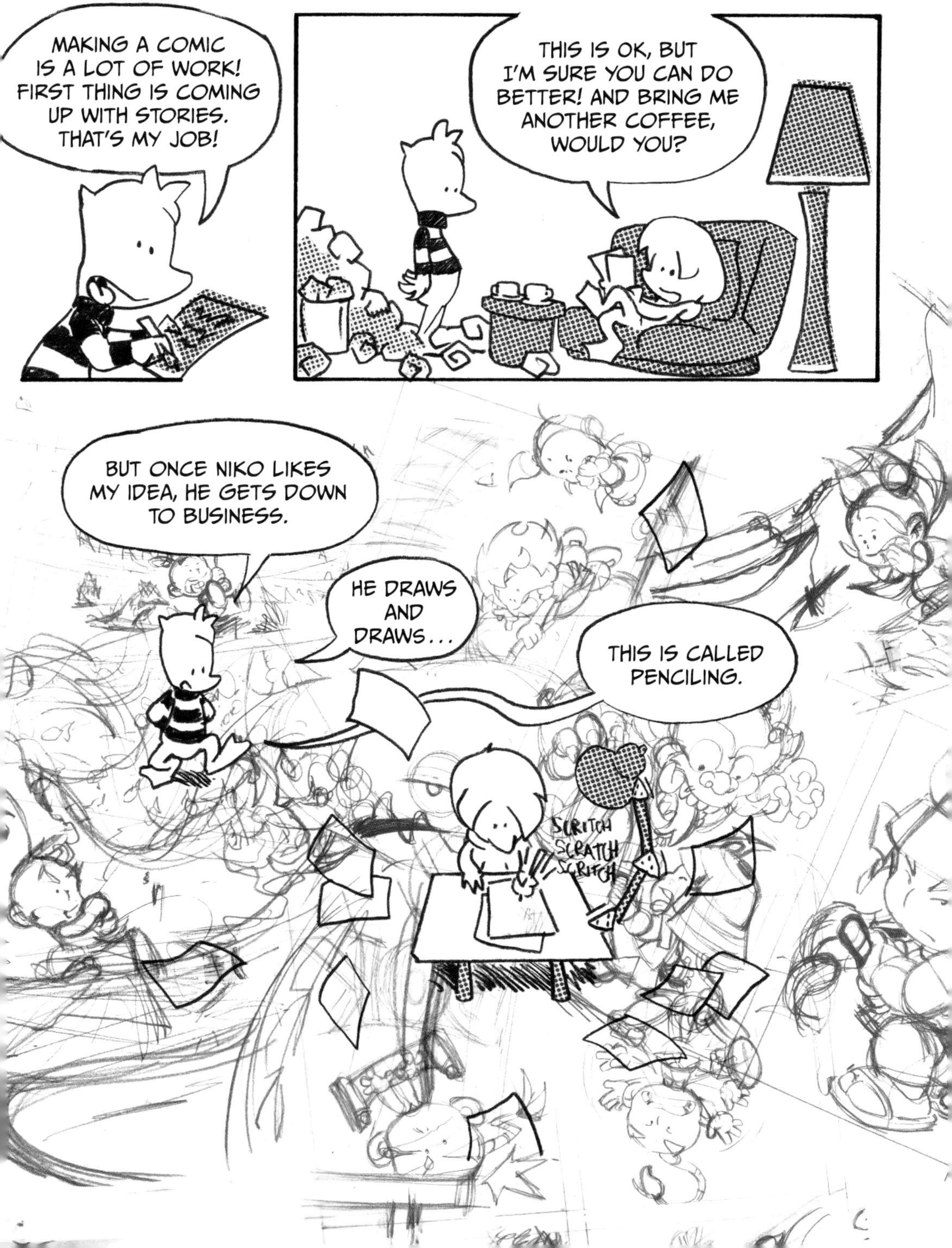
MAKING A COMIC IS A LOT OF WORK! FIRST THING IS COMING UP WITH STORIES. THAT'S MY JOB!
THIS IS OK, BUT I'M SURE YOU CAN DO BETTER! AND BRING ME ANOTHER COFFEE, WOULD YOU?
BUT ONCE NIKO LIKES MY IDEA, HE GETS DOWN TO BUSINESS.
HE DRAWS AND DRAWS...
THIS IS CALLED PENCILING.
SCRITCH
SCRATCH
SCRITCH

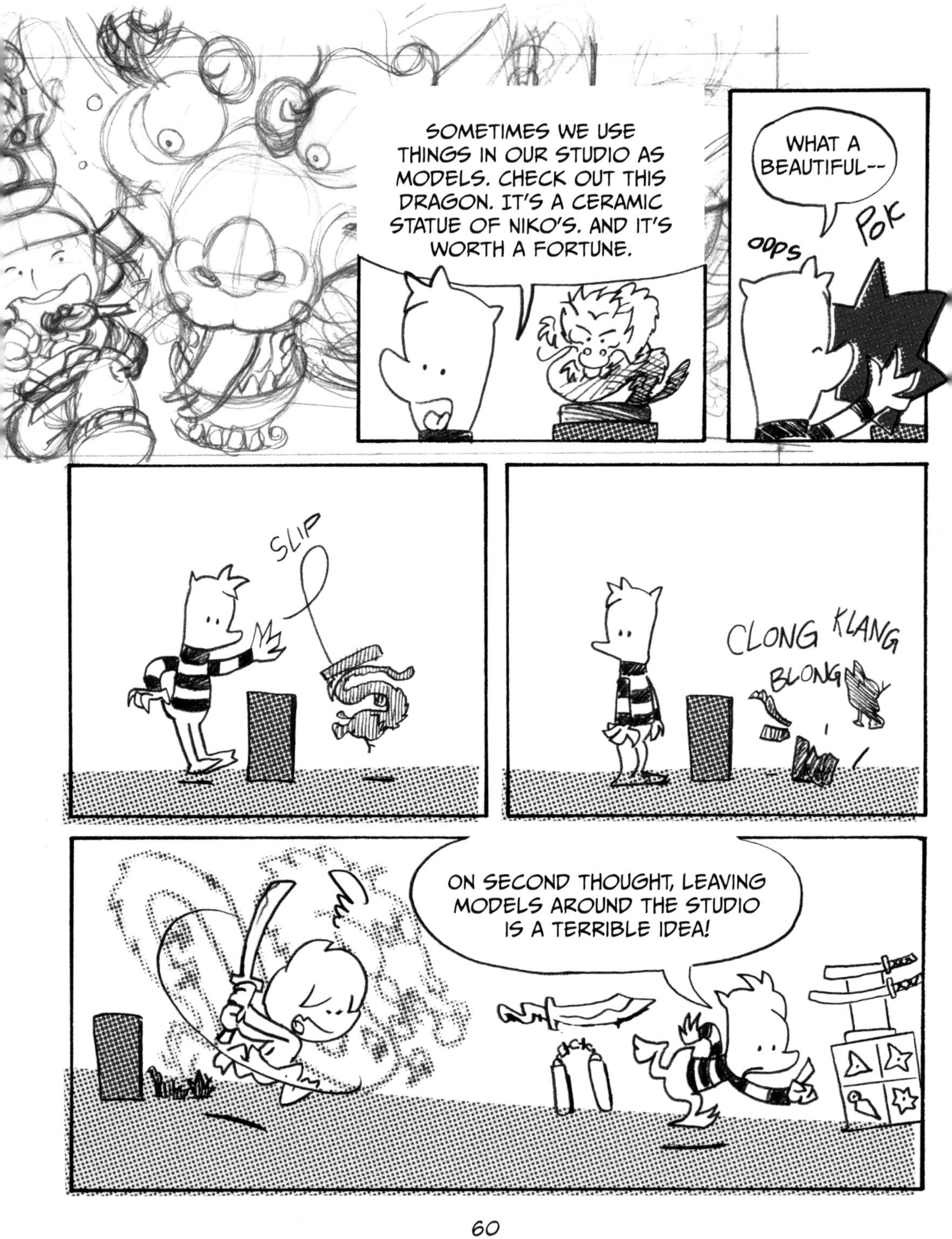
SOMETIMES WE USE THINGS IN OUR STUDIO AS MODELS. CHECK OUT THIS DRAGON. IT'S A CERAMIC STATUE OF NIKO'S. AND IT'S WORTH A FORTUNE.
WHAT A BEAUTIFUL--
OOPS
POK
SLIP
CLONG
KLANG
BLONG
ON SECOND THOUGHT, LEAVING MODELS AROUND THE STUDIO IS A TERRIBLE IDEA!

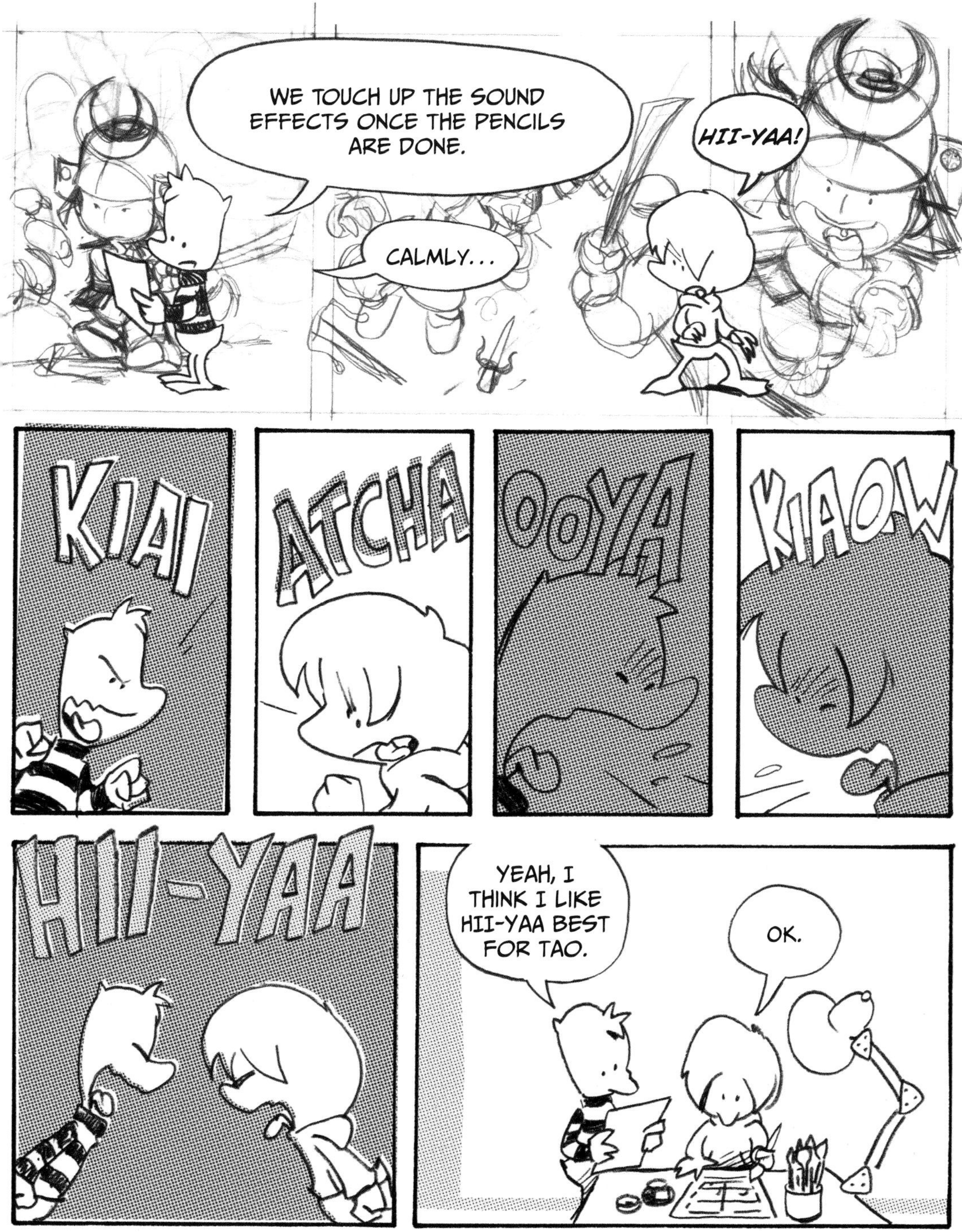
WE TOUCH UP THE SOUND EFFECTS ONCE THE PENCILS ARE DONE.
CALMLY...
HII-YAA!
KIAI
ATCHA
OOYA
KIAOW
HII-YAA
YEAH, I THINK I LIKE HII-YAA BEST FOR TAO.
OK.

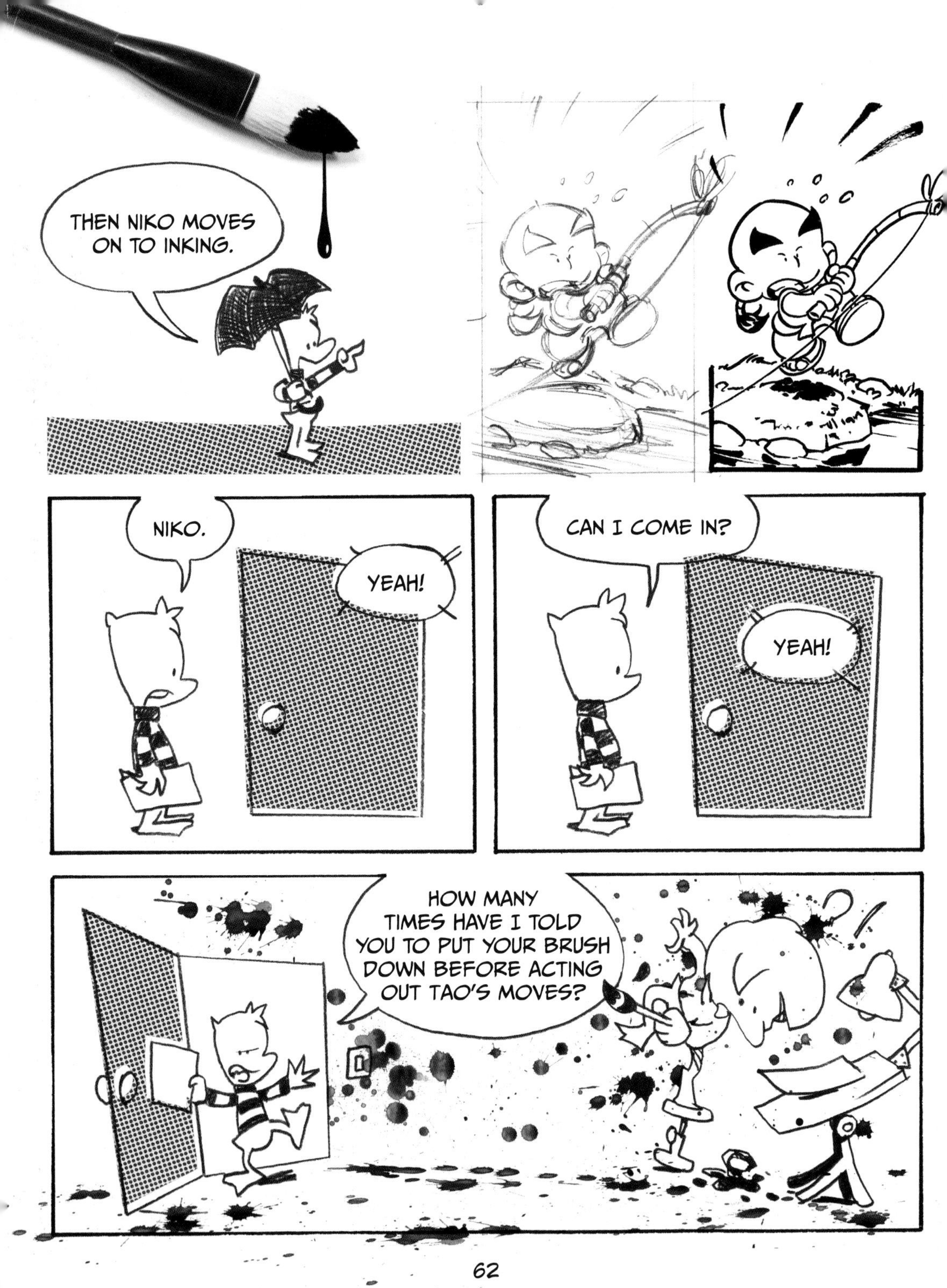
THEN NIKO MOVES ON TO INKING.
NIKO.
YEAH!
CAN I COME IN?
YEAH!
HOW MANY TIMES HAVE I TOLD YOU TO PUT YOUR BRUSH DOWN BEFORE ACTING OUT TAO'S MOVES?

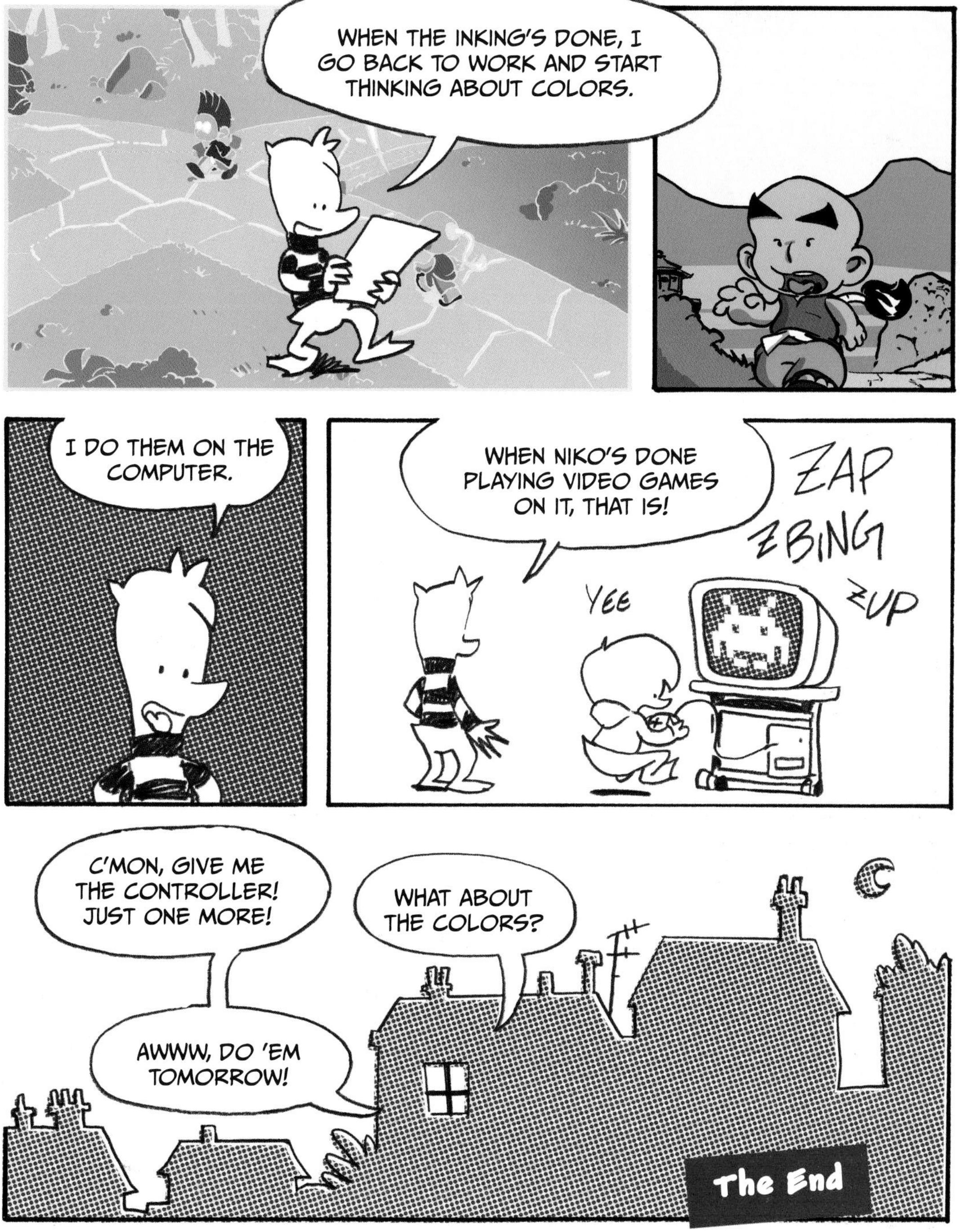
WHEN THE INKING'S DONE, I GO BACK TO WORK AND START THINKING ABOUT COLORS.
I DO THEM ON THE COMPUTER.
WHEN NIKO'S DONE PLAYING VIDEO GAMES ON IT, THAT IS!
ZAP
ZBING
ZUP
YEE
C'MON, GIVE ME THE CONTROLLER! JUST ONE MORE!
WHAT ABOUT THE COLORS?
AWWW, DO 'EM TOMORROW!
The End

TAO
The Little Samurai

#1 Pranks and Attacks!
#2 Ninjas and Knock Outs!
#3 Clowns and Dragons!